BIRDS
OF A FEATHER

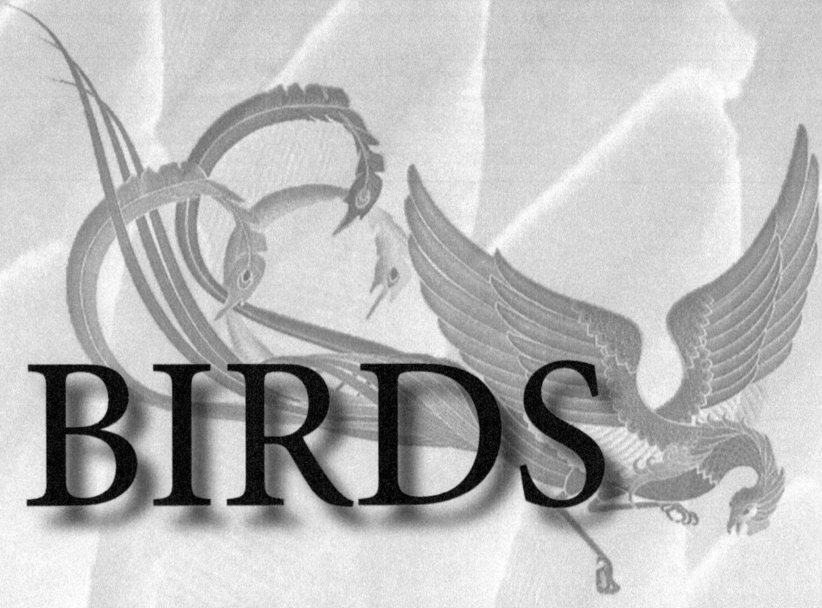

BIRDS

OF A FEATHER

By:

MICHELLE WALLACE CAMPANELLI

ARPress LLC
45 Dan Road Suite 5
Canton MA 02021
Hotline: 1(888) 821-0229
Fax: 1(508) 545-7580

Ordering Information:
Quantity sales. Special discounts are available on quantity purchases by corporations, associations, and others. For details, contact the publisher at the address above.

Printed in the United States of America.

ISBN-13:   Softcover   979-8-89330-197-7
           Hardcover   979-8-89330-199-1
           eBook   979-8-89330-198-4

Library of Congress Control Number: 2024901772

CONTENTS

For Louis,

For I am persuaded that neither death nor life,

Nor angels, nor principalities,

Nor things present, nor things to come,

Nor height, nor depth

Nor anything else in all creation,

Will be able to separate us from the love of God

In Christ Jesus our Lord.

Romans 8:38-39

Thank you, Fontaine Wallace, for being such a wonderful Mom and personal editor. Rachael Bindas and Lasheri Walls at Dorrance, thanks for your hard work that is very appreciated! Christopher Maslow, thank you for the cover art of a vulture, which I absolutely cherish!

CHAPTER 1

In the town where I live, palm trees line the block and sway to the cool breezes from the Atlantic Ocean. My neighbors smile and wave at several children jumping rope across the street. Palm Bay is known for being a great place to call home; it's not far from the beach and typically sunny.

You wouldn't think something so crazy would happen here, yet it did. My name is Officer Laura Camp. I'm a corrections officer. I've been working at the Juvenile Detention Center since I received my bachelor's degree in criminal justice from Florida State University. This is honestly the job I've always wanted. My husband even encouraged me to apply though corrections is typically a man's world. I knew I could do it though. I'm nearly six feet tall and can bench press over two hundred pounds. But the story I am about to tell isn't one of female empowerment but of my bizarre account of the most unusual killers.

Palm Bay is loaded with them. When they got infected, all hell broke loose. I'm not talking about the people. No, those who live here are good-hearted folks; some are locals but many transplants from the islands and retirees from the north reside. None of us ever expected to face what happened the year the space shuttle shot up for the last time in 2011.

That's when all these strange happenings began.

Here, we are used to seeing the most beautiful wildlife in the world, incredible preserves which protect some of Florida's endangered species, such as sandhill cranes, scrub jays, grasshopper sparrows, and the manatee. Near Turkey Creek, Suwannee, Cooter turtles and colorful fish swim in every stream.

We love our Florida wildlife and care for our creatures. For a while, we even found vultures a very important part of our ecosystems. There was no reason to worry. These birds nicknamed the "garbage collectors," sit perched on the top of lampposts or cell phone towers. Black as night they are. At first glance these creatures resemble a dark eagle or hawk until they turn around and stare with beady black eyes. Then the watcher realizes how huge and ominous the vultures are.

They clean the streets of our roadkill, everything from possum, armadillo, raccoon, and the occasional feral cat. Mostly, they are harmless to everything living, that is, at least until the accident—that's what the other officers were told; maybe what we believed for a while anyway.

I grew up here; I never feared a bird in my life. They leave humans alone, so I don't bother them. They want to take the squirrel that got smashed by a car to the side and peck away in groups—good for them. It's what God made them for.

Humans need garbage collectors.

We can't have rotting, disgusting creatures bleeding all over our paved streets. We simply forget that they are there; thanks to the vultures, our roadkill gets eaten. Once they spot something dead, they gather in groups and sit staring back at the cars as they roll past.

Children even smile and point at the sight of our Palm Bay vultures that love to fly in high circles in our sunny skies. Most of these children are too young to remember *The Birds* movie by Alfred Hitchcock, so what they see is something unique and doing its purpose for mankind.

We needed the Space Shuttle Program in our area, too. When *Atlantis* soared off into the cloudy sky for its last flight, none of the people of Palm Bay were happy about it. Most of Brevard County mourned the loss of one of the greatest NASA programs in our human history.

Three thousand people were about to be laid off, too, with not as many technical jobs vacant anymore. Space support companies were all moving to Texas. Good for them, but bad for Cape Canaveral and my town, Palm Bay. Florida would never quite be the same until Space X, and we knew it!

It was one of those soon-to-be-out-of-a-job workers from the Space United who decided revenge was in order instead of acceptance. I saw the whole thing with my own eyes, but at the time I didn't realize what I had witnessed.

In fact, I didn't think much of it at the time.

I was sitting in the juvenile detention van alongside my partner, and we were transporting two juvenile offenders to the Viera Courthouse. The van was parked at a red light when a man sped out of the Space United building carrying what appeared to be a silver wine bottle. He was being chased by two security guards in pursuit.

At the time, I almost laughed thinking that guy must really have what I call "a touch of the Jimmy Buffets." That means he had to party right now, escaping with the wine bottle at breakneck speed.

"Check that out," Officer Dirk said.

"I know. I see him. Two bucks says the skinny guard tackles him," I replied.

We watched the men chase the runner who tripped, causing the wine bottle to break and splash its contents into the retention water at the edge of the property by the road. It hadn't rained in so long that the water was barely six inches high.

As soon as the bottle broke, the two security guards stopped in their tracks and immediately covered their faces with their arms. A small bit of smoke escaped. The man who had once held that bottle like a Double-back wine stepped back with a horrified look on his face.

"Oh no!" he cried out. He yelled so loudly that I could hear it through the small opening of my door window.

Suddenly, a giant black bird flew through the smoke, swooped down over the man, and nearly knocked him over.

The man let out an awful scream. "Help!" he yelled, clearly afraid of the vulture. One of the security guards ran back to the building and pushed a red button on the outside wall which prompted an alarm like a high pitch screech. Swoosh! The vulture flew again over the water toward the man who had broken the bottle. Instantly, the man ran back toward the building just as the vulture snatched the bottle and flew upward, flapping its giant black wings.

"That was one big vulture!" announced my partner.

"What does he want with smoking wine?"

I watched the vulture continue to ascend toward a cell phone tower. Nearly a dozen more glared down over the road through their slit eyes. The one landed on top, turned around, and started crushing the bottle within its beak high above us, raining down glass shards to the dirt below.

I remember thinking how good it was that no one was standing underneath the tower. I didn't know then that this was just the beginning of a war between man and the winged beasts.

CHAPTER 2

When we got back to the facility, Officer Dirk and I escorted the two juveniles we had from court back inside the detention center. For the most part, the youths didn't cause many problems. A couple times they tried to speak to one another, but my partner made sure they kept their mouths closed and their shackled wrists tied tight. I had nearly forgotten that I had just seen a vulture fly off with a mouse in its clutches. That vulture didn't seem as bad as the two young gang members that Officer Dirk and I were keeping in line until we got them back to their 10' x 12' concrete cells. These two were from opposite gangs in the local neighborhood. One was nicknamed Crown, whose main purpose is to sell drugs on a certain corner lot not far from the university. The other gang was called the Union, a larger group of thugs who centered on the sale of sexual favors from prostitutes and boxing bouts. The leader of the Union owns a club in the worst part of town, far from the beachside communities and close to the railroad's tracks. Cheap tricks weren't the only thing the Union was known for. They had one very special boxer who, if he survived his next few weeks in our juvenile detention center, might even make it to a national heavyweight championship boxing match. At only seventeen years old, the pride of the Union was Jack "the Mack" Stubins who was just arrested for the fourth time for grand theft. He had stolen everything from Rolex watches to cars. However, now he's facing up to three years in adult prison for driving away in a Rolls Royce valued at over $150,000. The glass door slid open, and Dirk and I brought the two large males back inside. Quickly, I signed them in, and we walked them back to their cells, which were on opposite sides of each other. One twelve-inch-thick cement wall was keeping these two gang members from killing one another. Officer Dirk gave me a smile.

"Go, park the van, Camp; these two are in for the evening."

"Not so tough in chains, are they?" I said.

"You wouldn't say that in the ring." Jack "the Mac" snarled, interrupting.

"You ain't so tough without a badge." I could have mouthed off, but the kid had no idea that tomorrow he'd be shipped up to the adult prison. No more easy rides because he was a local celebrity. Jack "the Mac" was about to go to trial and serve real time instead of being one of the greatest boxers that had ever come out of our town.

"You won't be seeing another boxing match for some time," Officer Dirk tagged.

"Don't be so sure," he said, chuckling as his one platinum tooth shimmered.

"That tooth is more than this week's paycheck," Officer Dirk added.

"Now that the governor took 3 percent of our paycheck, yeah, I'd say it's worth a lot more."

Being in this JDC (Juvenile Detention Center) can be as hard on the corrections officers as it is for the prisoners who were dumb enough to commit serious crimes to be sent here. We are all in prison here; the only difference is that I get to go home to a nice, warm house to see my husband. These juveniles get to stare at four cement walls and sleep on a slab.

"How was court?" asked Captain McBride. She was standing in the doorway, and Captain McBride took up that entire space. Near six foot, four and 250 pounds, nobody but nobody messed with Captain McBride. She was one big momma that nobody would be crazy to cross.

"That truck kid behaves?" I knew she was referring to Jack "the Mack" since he is rumored to have a right-hand punch like being hit by a Mack truck.

"No problems," I responded.

"He's got a mouth on him," Officer Dirk finished, signing the checklist.

"I'm going to go fill the van with gas. I'll be right back." Officer Dirk scratched his head and strutted out of the glass enclosure. For a moment, I watched him. For an African American man with no hair, Officer Dirk was a very attractive. In fact, it was nearly impossible for most women not to notice him, especially Captain McBride.

"Sugar, you see tomorrow's docket?" Captain McBride asked.

"Full house," I replied.

"That boxing kid sure looks like a handful."

"He'll be leaving sometime tomorrow, and I don't think he realizes that they are making room for him next door." Captain McBride shook her head in disapproval. I knew that meant that he would be facing trial as an adult; even being a local celebrity won't get him out of this mess. It was probably better that he gets away from the Crown gang member across the hall, too. The last thing we need at JDC is a gang war.

"It's going to be a long day tomorrow, so get a good night's rest," Captain McBride suggested.

"I'm looking forward to it." I smiled.

"Your husband going to cook you something fine and dandy?" she asked me.

"Being a chef's wife has its perks."

"You've got to give me the recipe for those cookies you brought last Christmas," Captain McBride pressed.

"I am getting sick of asking."

"He said that they are a family restaurant secret."

"We all got our secrets!" Captain McBride moved her large frame closer. "Now get. I'll see you tomorrow."

"I've still got five minutes left on the clock."

"Get!" Captain McBride said, and then slowly she smiled. "Don't come back without that recipe and the one for chicken marsala."

Quickly, I rose to my feet and hurried to the glass door. Captain McBride from the Master Control opened the door. With a wave to Jack "The Mack," I exited the building and headed over to my RX-8 to drive home. Awe, home. I couldn't wait. The ride home was unremarkable. I opened my car door and heard the sound that always made me know I was right where I loved to be, the happy sound of my dog greeting me. Turning the key, I heard him scratching at the door. His yelps were gaining in speed and strength. The second the door shoved open, out jumped Doofus, the world's cutest dog. He was part poodle, the half that was smart; the other part was a Schnauzer, and we won't even mention the attitude. Black and brown, Doofus was my best friend right along with my husband of ten years. Coming around the corner, I saw him, and my heart jumped a beat. Every time I see Doofus, I remember how he got his name. I first saw him as a three-month-old puppy at the animal shelter. I had walked in with every intention of getting my friend Donna a kitten. I've known my best friend since junior high school, and we still get together to this day. It was Donna's birthday, and cats are her thing. Guitars and cats, that's what Donna loves most in this world, besides her husband and kids. She's got seven of them. So, to call her a cat lady is an understatement, although she's far from crazy. On her birthday, I got this bright idea to buy her another kitten, save one from being killed. Perhaps, she'd like one of these cats in jail. We went in with every intention of getting her a new pet, not me. Then I saw the puppy in the last cell. He looked up at me with the happiest looking eyes, and he was so tiny.

"Look at this little guy," I said to Donna as she was stuck looking at the kittens. Donna is quite beautiful, with short blonde hair and big blue eyes. She lifted her sunglasses and placed them above her forehead. "Oh my, that tail." I laughed when I saw the little tail or stub moving so fast.

"Now he's cute," Donna commented. An employee of the shelter walked over.

"You want to take him for a walk out back?" I should have said no. I wasn't looking to bring home a pet at all, but this little puppy with the dark, happy eyes—I just couldn't leave without just one little walk. He had so much energy, pacing back and forth by the gate, looking up at us, wagging his stubby tail so excitely.

"Go ahead," Donna said.

"I think I'll play with the kittens for a while." I took a look at three tiny strays in a kitten cage. One was black. One was white. Then the last one looked like it was wearing a tuxedo with white socks on. Donna began petting the white one. The mixed color one was the cutest, but Donna seemed to be drawn to the all-white one with big, green eyes.

"Looks like a cotton ball," I said. "This may be the closest thing to a snowflake we will see this year."

"You like him?"

"That one is a girl," said a shelter volunteer.

"Would you like to hold her?"

"Oh, yes!" Donna said.

"Would you like to take the schnoodle out?" the shelter employee asked me next. I should have said no, but in life, sometimes the biggest joys could have first been a no.

"Okay, but I am not looking for a pet right now."

The shelter employee handed Donna the white baby kitten and unlocked the cage of the puppy. She quickly put the dog in a harness and handed me the leash. I didn't have to tug on the rope to get this puppy to come to me. Instead of running for the yard, he tried to jump up on me, so I leaned down and picked him up. He just licked me about thirty times before he finally stopped. In my arms the puppy wiggled.

"My goodness. I think he likes you," said the shelter employee.

"I'd say that's a winner," Donna said, snuggling the kitten. I wasn't sure if she was talking about the kitten or puppy. Quickly, I placed the dog down and started walking toward the yard. He was right at my heels and pounced into the grass wagging his tail. He saw a lizard on the wall and jumped up at it.

"They can climb. Can't get him." The puppy continued to jump at it and bark. "Don't be a doofus," I said, trying to pull him into the grass. Any joy of being in the grass was gone. This dog wanted that lizard, and at the moment, that was all he wanted. So, I waited, watching the dog jump up and down, trying to scare the lizard half to death. Laughter exploded. It was a happy moment when the puppy finally turned around to get picked up again.

"So, are you taking that adorable Doofus puppy home?" Donna asked me.

"Are you taking home Snowflake?"

Together, we nodded as one in sync. We had both made the decision to bring home pets from the shelter at that very moment. Our hearts had been touched. Both had instantly become our friends, ones we never wanted to walk away from, just like their new masters.

"Do you think Louigi will like him?" I asked Donna. "Or will I be in a heap of trouble when I get home?"

"I think he'll love Doofus," Donna said. I knew she was right.

Louigi had a dog named Mittzy when he was growing up, which was a schnauzer, too. The genes were protective. Perhaps, Doofus thought he was saving me from being attacked by the lizard that was invading our space. Louigi would love him. I just knew it. It would be love at first sight. Just like it had been for me.

"I'll take him home," I told the shelter employee. She smiled.

"He's got all his shots, and he's free with a donation to the shelter."

"What about the kitten?"

"Same. Already spayed, too."

"We'll take both," Donna said.

"They will both be going to very loving homes."

"Great! I'll start the paperwork," the shelter employee said.

That day, I opened my wallet and donated everything I had to the shelter. When I got home, Louigi was shocked. For a moment, he looked a little angry. But before he could finish saying

"You got a dog without checking with me first…" Doofus was in his arms licking his face as he had done with me earlier.

"Okay," Louigi said after a long licking. "Doofus can stay."

CHAPTER 3

The smell of chicken parmesan engulfed my senses as I sneaked up behind my handsome husband. He was naked from the waist up, and every inch of his tan, muscular Italian frame excited me. At the moment, he looked far more delicious than dinner.

"How was work?" he asked, his back still turned to me.

"Same ol', same ol'. Captain McBride wants that cookie recipe," I answered. His deep chuckle warmed my heart as I wrapped my arms around his waist. My fingers tumbled down his six pack stomach muscles and rose past the spiffs of hair around his small brown nipples.

"I read in the paper that Jack 'The Mack' was arrested yesterday. Have you seen him yet?" He was sniffing for more information.

"You know I can't talk specifics."

"He's extremely dangerous. Did you see what he did in his last fight? Mahoney didn't even last fifteen seconds in the ring with him."

Quietly, he shyly backed away, turned, and then loaded two plates with pasta and sauce-covered chicken. He headed toward the back porch; I noticed that he had set a small table in the garden for dinner. Right in the center of hibiscus trees, firecracker, and princess plants sat an intimate table with two chairs near the bird feeder. Noting that the feeder was empty of sunflower seeds, I bent over, grabbed the plastic bag of feed from underneath the sink, and followed him out.

"I was wondering why I hadn't seen any blue jays this morning," he announced. "The squirrels must be hungry."

"No hungrier than I am," I replied as I filled the bird feeder and dropped the heavy sack. The wind was blowing so hard, I worried my hair looked something like the Bride of Frankenstein. He handed me a spoon and a napkin. Honestly, I can never get used to eating pasta with a spoon. Half the time, twirling never brings the pasta to my mouth, yet I tried my best because, indeed, my stomach was growling.

"Your sunflowers are finally opening," he alerted me. Glancing over to the nearly five-foot sunflowers, I proudly smiled.

"So, are you taking extra precautions at work since you have a boxing celebrity?"

"I can't talk about specifics," I reminded, straightening and forcing the melancholy from my voice. "You know that."

"Mack's there. Where else would they take someone under eighteen in Brevard? Trust me, tell me what's going on. Are they going to adjudicate him? He's old enough to be tried as an adult, and he has the championship boxing match scheduled soon."

"You don't even like boxing," I countered.

"How's your dinner?" he diverted my attention. I took a bite. The chicken was hot but absolutely delicious. His homemade sauce had a hint of sweetness; he must have added some sugar and what tasted like a hint of oregano and basil.

"Is the basil from the garden?"

"I dried them in the sun," he smiled. What a gorgeous smile he had. I studied my husband's face, with its solid features and chiseled jawline. His hair was long and curly, reaching to his shoulders. Wavy ringlets perfectly framed his Italian appearance. "You would not believe how much time I spend trying to find the perfect basil for you."

"How'd I get so lucky, Louigi, to have you in my life?" He leaned over and kissed my lips.

"Ouch." He jumped back. "Your badge got me." He chuckled, showing me where the top of my shield had scratched his bare skin. His muscular build caught my attention. Quickly, I removed my silver star and grabbed him in my arms. His lips took mine, and I immediately forgot about the chicken and any gravy he had created. This man was all I wanted to taste against my lips; we kissed in the garden as the sun was starting to set. The birds of paradise flowers swayed in the light Florida breeze as he picked me up and carried me over to the hammock tied between two queen palms. I loved seeing the flicker in his eyes when he looked at me. For several minutes we kissed, with my arms wrapping around his tan frame.

"Glad we got the fence," he chuckled.

"So glad," I agreed, trying to kiss him again.

"I should put the food back in the fridge." He remembered. "Just give me a moment."

"No," I begged. Despite my plea, he turned toward the table to grab the leftovers before the bugs got them. He glanced back over his shoulder and smiled at me as he carried the plates inside. This seemed like paradise until something big and black landed near the birdfeeder in between the bag of seed and the table. I'd never seen one so close before; this giant bird had red in its eyes and white drool at its mouth. I sat up in the hammock. It almost seemed that the vulture was eyeing me for his next dinner. Impossible! Vultures only go after the dead. Right? I watched him stare back at me, and then he hopped twice toward the bag of seed. He pecked at it a few times and then pulled out a giant cockroach. There definitely was something different about this bird. Could it have been the same giant vulture that had swooped down for the bottle at Space United? It looked sick. Why were its eyes so red, and what was that dripping from its beak? Was that blood dripping from its nose?

"Get out of here!" screamed my husband. He was holding a broom and shooing it away with broad strokes. "Go!" The vulture just sat there, staring at him.

"Leave him be, Louigi!" I jumped up from the hammock and dashed over to my husband. Slowly, together, we backed away toward the glass patio doors to enter our house.

"What's wrong with that bird? Did you see its eyes?" Louigi gasped as he locked the door behind us.

"I don't know."

Suddenly, the bird flew at our glass door! Bang! It crashed hard and cracked it. Shaking its head, it dropped, then hopped away, and stared at Doofus with a dazed look in its eyes.

"It's got rabies!" Louigi gasped and opened the door. "Go, Doofus!" As our dog rushed past the bird, the vulture snapped at the shoulder. Doofus leapt to the left and rushed into the house.

"They don't get rabies," I reminded as we hurried inside, and I shut the door. "No, this bird has something wrong with it. I better alert animal control."

Louigi and I moved through the kitchen, and I grabbed the phone on the wall. While I dialed the number, I heard another bang against the glass door. This time the bird hit harder, making the crack larger as the sunset sparkled across the pane. My husband looked horrified as the bird shook back to its feet and flew away in two big swoops.

"Animal control. How can we be of service?" a voice answered.

"That thing is gone, right?" He nodded his head as if he was still in shock. I hung up.

"It just flew away," he muttered. "What the hell was wrong with that vulture?" he repeated.

"It looked like it wanted to attack us!"

I put down the phone and hugged my husband. At over six foot, two and packed with muscles, it was the only time I had ever seen him so afraid that he was trembling in my arms. Right now, he needed me, and there was nothing animal control could do to fix him or my glass door. Doofus padded to the glass door and yelped.

CHAPTER 4

Officer Dirk took Jack into Captain McBride's office. His hands and feet were cuffed, so he made a loud crashing noise when he sat in the chair opposite of her desk. The captain glanced over at Officer Dirk and smiled.

"How has your shift been so far, Dirk?" she asked him.

"Better, since you called me into your office," he winked. Jack chuckled.

"That looks like some misbehaving going on up in here juvie jail."

"Mind your business." Captain McBride glared at Jack. "We've been friends a long time, Dirk and me. We don't take kindly to kids that are born with a silver spoon in their mouth and got the world on a string." Jack's eyes squinted in disbelief.

"You don't know me."

"Watch your mouth." Officer Dirk moved a paper over from by the captain to across the table along with a pen. "Sign that; we gave you this, so you'll know the rules and what we expect from you." Jack picked up the paper, which was stapled in two.

"Only fifteen-minute showers?"

"We provide the soap." Officer Dirk chuckled.

"You watch, too, or is Big Momma here more your thang?" Jack said. Officer Dirk moved closer and leaned down.

"You watch that mouth, Mack, or you will be sleeping on cement. I'll take away the mat."

"Cements got no cushion," Captain McBride added. "Not like those big old beds with box springs and fluffy pillows."

"I don't think he gets a pillow tonight, Cap."

"We got to do this? Be all mean cop to the criminal. I've done nothing to either one of you. You have no idea who I am or where I've come from."

"I bet it's the same ol' story I hear every day," Captain McBride said. "You were just bored and didn't think the owner would mind if you stole the Rolls out the garage. Just having some fun—didn't mean to cause any problems or trouble with the police."

"I heard he's a chip off the ol' block," Officer Dirk said. "His father is up at the state pen for murder."

"I ain't nothing like my pops."

"Who's his daddy?"

"You mean, you didn't know? It's all over the news about his father trying to get to attend the boxing championships. A lawyer is trying to work it out so that he can see his son get the belt he trained him to wear."

"That's what's on the news?" Jack asked. "It ain't like that. I don't even want him there. I don't want to ever see him again!" Officer Dirk was taken back by that response. Jack was mad.

"Damn it! Why is he trying to ruin everything for me? I don't want the world to know that my pops is a con."

"What are you saying? Didn't you just steal a Rolls out your neighbor's garage?" Captain McBride scoffed.

"If you don't like cons, why are you trying so hard to be one?"

"It's not like that. You don't know me or my pops. You don't know what he's like or what he expects from me."

"So, he proud of you for stealing that car or for being considered one of the most dangerous gang members we have on the Space Coast?"

"You already think you know me."

"I've seen too many of these gang members from both sides of the city come in here thinking they are the baddest of the bad. You want to see bad. Try being a mother for a day and see if you don't break down." Officer Dirk came around the desk and put his hand on her shoulder.

"It's okay. He doesn't know about Douglas." The captain's eyes welled up.

"Every day I come in here and meet one of you from this gang or that gang. You drop out of school. Get drug addicted. Do crime and then expect sympathy from us that you've had it rough. So, your dad is a criminal. Tough break, kid. You didn't have to follow in his footsteps. You were the one that decided to cross the line between what is right and what is wrong. You did. So now you're here, and you're my mess."

Jack asked, "Who's Douglas?"

"Don't you mention his name! You got no right!" Captain McBride snapped.

"Sorry," Jack suddenly said, focusing his attention on Officer Dirk's sympathetic face. "I can see whoever he is must mean a lot to you."

"My son, Douglas Bobby McBride, seven years old and he's got cancer. You think the world owes you something. Well, it don't. So, Jack the Mack, you are going to behave when you are here and follow those rules. Do you hear me?"

Jack shifted in his chair, and instead of being sarcastic or rude, he said, softly, "Yes, ma'am. You won't have no trouble from me. Sorry to hear about your little boy. Is Douglas going to be all right?"

"The children's hospital is giving me hope," Captain McBride said.

"He's the sweetest thing you ever saw," Officer Dirk said. His gaze softened.

"I'm sorry," Jack said.

"My momma died of breast cancer two years ago, and that's when my pops went crazy. He was always violent to her, but you should have seen him when she was dying. Never left her side. Crying like a baby, he did, all day and night. Begging God to save her and he'd be a good man."

"You shouldn't have brought that up to someone whose only son has cancer," Officer Dirk said.

"Not trying to be disrespectful, but I know. It ain't easy seeing someone you love get cancer. He's only seven? Yeah, you are right. Life ain't fair. It ain't fair to me or you, Captain. But here we are, stuck together like glue until my trial. You won't get any trouble from me, but there are other gang members in here who wouldn't mind me dead. So, you better watch my back in here. I don't have eyes in the back of my head."

"I do." Officer Dirk watched Jack sign the paper in front of him. "You're my responsibility in here."

"And mine," Captain McBride said. "Just follow the instructions on that form, and you won't have any trouble in juvie."

CHAPTER 5

Jack stood trying to triangulate his position. In such a small room, he looked big. Officer Dirk stood close to him.

"Time to get back to your cell for nighty night."

"Lights out at nine, I read." Jack nodded, then walked around his chair, and headed for the door. His chains made lots of noise as he walked down the blank hallway. Once Officer Dirk and he entered the cell wing, out came hoots and hollers from the other juveniles in the cells. Lots of muttering circulated down the halls. Officer Dirk listened. At first the comments were supportive.

"You're gonna win that championship, Mack!"

"You got this," said another. "You're a badass."

Then came a warning from someone Officer Dirk recognized as a Union gang member. "Watch yourself around the Crowns. Bart is in cell two down from you."

"Can't do much in a cell," Jack said underneath his breath.

"They take us out in the yard together," the fellow Union gang member said. Officer Dirk grimaced.

"Shut up and go to bed, Miles."

"Just trying to help my brother," said Miles. His choppy brown hair had a derelict, unkept appearance. "You better watch him in the yard." Officer Dirk stopped.

"Have you heard of a plan?" Jack stopped and stood next to Officer Dirk. "When?"

"Tomorrow in the yard. That Crown with the skull tattoo on his arm. Shank ya."

"You heard this from who?" Officer Dirk questioned. Jack leaned in and hummed tunelessly.

"Tell him."

"The one in the cell next to him. They are both Crowns, and they want to prove they can take down the Union's boxer. They are trying to prove something big. Send a message to our side of the city." Jack glanced over at Officer Dirk.

"Can you move me over to this part? I need to stay away from them if you want no trouble."

Officer Dirk said, "I'll see what I can do to move you. For now, go back to 114." Jack nodded.

"Thanks."

"Move him next to me," said Miles with a wink. "I can protect him."

"Juvie is not a war zone for Union and Crowns. Got it?" Officer Dirk said. "Get moving, Jack."

"His nickname is Mack. Cause he hits like a Mack truck," said Miles. "He's the greatest boxer in this state. If he wanted, he could kill you with one punch. So, you better watch yourself, Pig."

"Shut up," Jack said to Miles with his gold tooth glistening by the moonlight streaming through the windows. "I need to get out of here to make the ring. I don't want no trouble in here."

"The Union will get you out, one way or another," Miles said. "To them boxing is as addictive as crack cocaine, and you're Prince."

"Is that a threat to break Jack out?" Officer Dirk asked. "Is it?"

"Not saying another word." Miles smiled. "Mack told me to shut up." Mack began to walk again, and Officer Dirk immediately trailed him. As they continued down the hallway, more shouts could be heard.

"You're our champ!"

"Love you, Mack!"

"Next Friday the belt is all yours!"

It wasn't until they approached the cells where the Crowns were did the tone change. In the cell next to Jack's was a guy twice his size. He was young, thin, and had a tattoo of a crown on his shoulder. In fact, that was the easiest way to figure out they were in the Crown gang. Each member had a crown tattoo. They could be anywhere on them, the arm, shoulder, leg, or even face, but they always had the tattoo. It was part of the Crown's initiation. The other part was that you had to be a drug dealer on the east side of the city.

"Enjoy your last night alive," he said softly.

"What did you just say?" Officer Dirk said. "You want the hole tonight?"

"You got rules," he said. "First you take away my mattress; then it's the hole."

"What's the hole?" Jack asked the Crown member.

"Solitary. It's not in the ground, but it's dark in there."

"You think a Crown or Union member is gonna care about being in the dark?" Jack questioned Officer Dirk.

"It would be better for us to miss lunch or something." The Crown member giggled, which made his large pot belly shake. Then his dark eyes tightened. "My name's Bart. And I am gonna kill you tomorrow."

Officer Dirk opened Jack's cell and began to remove Jack's handcuffs quickly. "I'll talk to Cap about moving you. Just wait here." Jack entered his cell. His eyes never moved away from Bart's. Jack wasn't about to be intimidated by a member of the opposite gang.

"I'll be right back." Officer Dirk shut the door and locked it.

"Nothing you can do will save him," Bart said through closed teeth.

"He's toast." Jack then nodded to Officer Dirk. "Better move me to the right side of juvie. The left side is not my people." Officer Dirk hurried down the hallway and into Captain McBride's office.

"What's the matter?" she immediately asked.

"We need to move Jack from 114 to 92. His cell is right next to two Crown members, and he's Union. They are threatening to kill him."

"Will this crap ever end?" Captain McBride whirled around and pulled out a folder in her desk. She wrote down the number 92 and crossed out 114 on the piece of paper. "Okay, move him. We don't need the trouble. Jack doesn't seem as horrible as the others."

"I know," Officer Dirk said. "He's not going to back down from a fight, though, so we better do what we can to keep the Union separated from the Crowns."

"We shouldn't care if they killed each other. Bad taking out the trash, yet then I wouldn't be doing my job. Would I? Looks like that Mack kid had a rough childhood, too. Let's do our best to keep him alive until his boxing match."

"He may need to go to the adult jail next door," Officer Dirk said. "If this keeps up. We don't need a riot."

"I thought you were into that sort of thing." The Captain chuckled. Officer Dirk bit his lower lip.

"Not tonight, pretty lady."

CHAPTER 6

The next morning, I woke next to my husband. His CPAP machine expelled air as he peacefully slept. Quickly, I checked the red mark on his chest my badge had dug in the night before; he was fine. No scratch or bruise appeared. I shut off the alarm at 4:45 a.m. It would have been blaring in fifteen minutes anyway. Yawning, I rose from underneath the black satin sheets and headed toward the bathroom. For the past four years I've been working at the JDC facility, but I never got used to having to wake up this early. Every week I look forward to Saturdays and Sundays when there isn't court so I could sleep in. I felt movement beside me. Louigi took off his mask. His voice held more than a hint of seduction, "Good morning, beautiful."

Surprised, I rolled over and stared at the strong angles of his handsome face. "You want me to move the alarm to eight o'clock, or do you not want to go back to sleep?"

"I think I'm up. You want breakfast?'

"I'll just grab something in the breakroom. I want to go in early to make sure Dirk did all right."

"You mean if Jack the Mack behaved himself?" Louigi asked while giving me a quick kiss on the lips that sent warm butterflies to my belly.

"I can't talk specifics. You know that."

"That's okay. I can sense you are worried." I leaned in and kissed him again, wanting another.

"How'd I get so lucky?"

"Nice. Change of subject. But since you did, I am the lucky one."

"Are you? Every day you have to worry if I will come home," I reminded.

"True. But you wouldn't be happy doing anything else. Wearing a badge is in your blood. I couldn't see you doing anything else than being an officer, unless you were in forensics. You love solving the crime with clues." My head hit the pillow.

"You know why I got in law. I wish it was a different story."

"Don't think about that," Louigi reminded, slinging his arm around his pillow. "I worry when you do that you think I'm going to do something like it."

I closed my eyes, fighting back the tears. "It makes me realize how blessed I am to have a man like you as my soulmate."

"I would never do to you what your father did to your mother."

"I know," I said. "You know that was both one of the worst moments and one of the best moments of my life."

"Best moment?"

"That's when I decided which side I'd be on."

"That Darth Vader moment?" I chuckled, then kissed his cheek. I relished the feel of his small facial hairs prickling my skin.

"Yes, the moment Vader asked me to go to the Dark Side of the Force, and I knew I wouldn't even though he was my father."

"I'm just glad you handled things in the way you did."

When Mom picked me up from elementary school early, she had no idea that her sick kid coming home sooner than expected would destroy her life. I knew something was wrong by the noises coming out of her bedroom. I thought someone was hurting my father, believe it or not. He was crying out like in pain. I was just a kid. I didn't know about sex then. My mother might have thought the same thing because she didn't stop the second we walked in the apartment. She might have thought those noises were him getting hurt too. Because when she went for the gun in the top draw of the kitchen buffet, she had no hesitation. She called back to me to call the police. Then those noises stopped. My father must have heard that just as she opened the door.

"You don't have to keep reliving this," Louigi reminded me.

"I know, but sometimes I feel like I need to. It reminds me how lucky I am to have you as my husband. It's why I would never hurt you either. This experience is also why I know deep down that even good people can kill even what they love most in this world."

"Really?'

"When Mom opened that door, that gun was pointed right at my dad and that mistress of his. You know, you'd think a mistress would be beautiful and skinny, the exact opposite of what my mom was. She wasn't. Miranda was overweight and not even pretty like my mom. Luckily, they were under a blanket, because that image of them together would have forever cemented in my memory."

Miranda screamed, 'Who is that?'

"Even as a child, I knew what my father was doing. I had seen it on television. He was having an affair and hadn't even been honest with the woman that he was married to. My father had taken down all our pictures on the wall. They were in a pile on the buffet."

"My mother shouted something about killing him for cheating on her. The woman jumped out of bed, screaming. She was a very large woman and absolutely horrified. She really thought my mom was about to kill him. She looked right at me. I'll never forget those eyes of Miranda. It was pure terror. She thought she was next."

"I didn't know," she kept screaming.

"Please, don't kill me. Look! Your little girl." Mom glanced over at me, but it wasn't anger I saw any more but total devastation.

"How long?" was her next question.

"How long has this been going on?"

"Two weeks," Miranda answered.

"I swear I didn't know he was with anybody else."

"I'm his wife of ten years," my mom told her.

"This is his daughter."

"I didn't know. I wouldn't have if I knew," Miranda told her.

"Then Miranda did something I didn't ever expect.

"I'll kill him myself. Hand me the gun."

"It was probably a trick to get your mom to hand her the gun," Louigi said.

"Maybe." I nodded.

"My mom waved the gun at her to leave. Miranda quickly grabbed her clothes, slapped the hell out of my dad, and then bolted naked out of my house. I thought for sure my dad was a goner by the look in my mom's face. That was the moment I realized even the best of people could turn in a moment of rage. I honestly wondered if my sweet little mom who tucked me in with a kiss every night was going to kill my dad, so I begged her myself to put the gun down. I was crying and begging for her not to hurt my father. I honestly think that was the only reason she didn't pull the trigger. She looked at me and then slowly put the gun back down. My father gasped with relief. He knew she could have pulled that trigger and thought the better of it."

"Thank you," he said to my mother.

"Get out, was the last thing she said to him." I wiped my eyes.

"He had never been much of a father and not much of a husband to my mom, but I didn't know then how hard life would be without a father."

"So, that was the moment when you decided to wear a badge to stop things like that?"

"Yes, now I better get to work." I rose from the bed and headed for the bathroom. In truth, I liked my job, but I really wanted to be a crime scene investigator and work with the city instead. Looking in the mirror, I slipped on my dark blue uniform picturing what I would look like in a white CFS jacket instead. Someday? It was my husband who went to church on Sundays to teach Sunday school anyways.

After I put on a little makeup and tied my hair back into a ponytail, I rushed into my Mazda RX-8 and began to drive to work. My car was a masterpiece of engineering, sporty, and with a powerful BOSE sound system that could earn me sound ordinance tickets if I so desired. These wheels were bad to the bone. It took nearly an hour on I-95 to get to the JDC facility right off of the 208 at St. John's exit, which winded down Grissom Road to Camp.

When I first started working there, I thought it was odd that my married last name was the same as the road that led to where I worked. However, Camp Road was no summer camp—that's for sure. If you lived off of Camp Road, you were virtually an inmate in one of the many state jails. Florida's governor had closed the one right across from the JDC. Five hundred correctional officers had lost their jobs in the depressed economy the new president promised to fix. In the meantime, a lot of my friends were losing their homes, and every day I worry if the next facility the governor would close would be mine.

Being an employee of the state of Florida used to stand for good benefits, pensions, excellent insurance, and retirement plans. Now every single one of us officers wonders when our jobs will be cut next. Rumor has it our JDC facility may close next year, and all the juveniles will be sent to a wing at the adult prison—kids in jails right next to child predators. That's the governor's big plan. With the economy in shambles and gas nearly four bucks a gallon on some days, I really should go back to college to become a CSI officer. There are always crimes that need to be solved! Plus, I wouldn't have to see the worst of the worst offenders, mouthing off all the time, thinking they are all badasses. What they really need are strong parents to keep them in line, with lots of drug or mental health counseling.

I parked my Mazda and headed toward the front, and I hit the buzzer. "Good morning, Sunshine," came Captain McBride's voice through the outdoor speaker. I heard the doors click, and I opened them only two feet later to be greeted by giant glass doors. Captain McBride nodded to me from the control center and buzzed me in. The glass doors opened, and I walked into another day on the job. From the control center, I signed the captain's sheet and recorded the time I arrived. "You're five minutes early," Captain McBride commented.

"How was it last night?"

"Jack 'the Mack' didn't sleep much," Captain McBride said. "I took his mat away because he tried to talk to another gang member."

"They never learn." I sighed.

"Other than that, it was a pretty quiet night."

"My house was attacked by a giant vulture last night," I explained. "I've never seen anything like this bird. It had giant red eyes."

"I would say it could be rabies, but vultures can't get rabies," Captain McBride responded. "In fact, they won't eat a raccoon off the road if it has it. They have something internal that tells them not to eat anything with a disease. How they know, I can't guess."

"There's one like that outside in the yard," Officer Dirk mentioned as he walked in and took the sign-in sheet from my hands.

"Huge one."

"They normally travel in groups," Captain McBride replied.

"You should see it." Officer Dirk signed his name and then hung the board back on the peg near the doorway.

"How many we got for court today?" Captain McBride pulled out the manifest and studied it for a moment. "You have three in the morning and maybe two reprimands in the afternoon."

"It's going to be another long one." Officer Dirk sighed.

"Should I keep the kids out the yard?" Captain McBride didn't respond. She suddenly rose and headed out of the control center. Quickly, she walked down the hallway past the administrative offices to the door that leads to the outside yard. Curiosity got the better of me, and I followed her. Officer Dirk did the same while he began eating an egg sandwich. He took a big bite, nearly finishing his breakfast in one massive gulp.

"Oh my!" Captain McBride gasped. Her over six foot and muscular frame nearly covered the entire window. "That is a big one."

I leaned over to see around her. Sure enough, in the only tree outside in the yard right above the half basketball court sat a giant black vulture with a small gray head and beady red eyes. It squawked at us. Officer Dirk put in the code to the door and threw out the rest of his egg sandwich.

"Now he'll eat and go away." The bird swooped down and sniffed what was a little bit of egg, sausage, and a part of a biscuit.

"That's generous of you to give your breakfast away." Captain McBride smiled at Officer Dirk.

"They were two for one this morning. I already ate one." Officer Dirk watched the bird continue to move his beak right above the sandwich. For a moment, the three of us just hung out by the window waiting for the bird to eat what would have been considered an excellent meal for a bird. The vulture instead stared at the biscuit and didn't take a bite.

"What the hell is wrong with that thing?" Captain McBride pondered.

"The one last night acted crazed. It nearly tried to break down my glass patio door."

"Why doesn't it eat?" Captain McBride squinted.

"And what's that? Blood coming out its mouth."

I couldn't see what she did without my glasses on, which were in my pocket. Slowly, I placed them on my face. With a big swoosh, the bird flew back up to the tree, leaving the half sandwich untouched.

"Better keep the kids out of the yard," I suggested. With the glasses on, it became clearer that there was something very wrong with that bird. White pus seemed to ooze out of his beak. In fact, it looked a lot like the same bird from last night.

"Maybe we should call animal control," Captain McBride said.

"Those kids don't get but an hour of sunshine."

"I'll make the call." Officer Dirk walked away, leaving me next to my boss.

"Hope the world's not coming to an end"—Captain McBride laughed— "when a bird like that becomes top priority around here. We got our own vultures of society to take care of, don't we?" I didn't answer. I realize these juveniles are criminals, but to call them the same thing as a bird like that, didn't seem right. Staring at that hideous beast—I thought it just didn't seem right.

CHAPTER 7

t didn't take long for animal control to arrive. A lanky teenager and a sun-leathered man in his late forties walked into the facility wearing white uniforms and visitor tags. The older man carried a tranquilizer gun in one hand while the boy held a giant net that looked like something from a pool supply company.

"Vultures can't get rabies," the man announced to Captain McBride, who stepped out of the master control booth to walk him down the hallway. Waiting at the door to let them out, I overheard the conversation about how vultures can sense if dead animal had rabies, and that's the only dead animal they won't consume. He warned to avoid any animal that the buzzards rejected.

"I don't care what the winged thing has; I just don't want him overlooking the yard with the kids out there," Captain McBride responded. By the time they reached my side, the vulture had moved from the fence to the basketball hoop. Blood was dripping from its beak. Clearly, the bird was sick.

"Lovely," the middle-aged man commented snidely, rubbing the back of his neck. Reading his name tag,

"Nice bird, Peter?"

"Peter Miller," he finished with a placating tone.

"I had a bird like this at my house last night, and it nearly broke my glass patio door," I commented.

"How much experience do you have as an animal control officer?" He straightened his glasses and scoffed.

"I've been in this business for over twenty years. I wrestle gators. You think a bird is tough? Now, he is a big one. I might need to take two shots, but I won't need to get close. I'll shoot 'em and take 'em to be tested. It'll cost you a hundred bucks."

"Cost us?"

"You think that's bad. It's fifty-five for a raccoon, and don't even ask about a gator." He chuckled.

"Not my bill." I unlocked the door, glancing down at the young man. He wasn't very tall, but his features looked a lot like the older one. Watching the bird, his eyes widened, and he gulped hard.

"Stay here, son," the older man ordered, gulping back a wobble in his voice.

"After he's down, come bring me the net."

"Okay," he murmured.

"The boy can't remain in the facility unsupervised," I said.

"I called and asked the captain if I could bring Jake in so he would see what happens to boys who don't go to school. He thinks my job is all easy and that there's no need to get a diploma."

"I see," I smiled.

"Scared straight kind of thing."

"Is it true that Jack the Mack is here?" the boy asked me.

"Not now, Jake," his father corrected.

"Come on, Dad, it was on the news that he got arrested for stealing a Rolls Royce!"

"Keep an eye on him while I take down the bird, Officer. I'm going to put it into a gilded cage for animal control to examine with a fine-tooth comb." He didn't look like much trouble compared to the kids I normally have to deal with.

"He's really a good boy, and this will only take a minute," the father tagged.

"We've got to get the kids in the yard before lunch. If the temperature hits over 90 degrees, they aren't permitted outside."

"It won't take but a minute. Honest!" He walked out the door and crouched down like an approaching puma. Out came his tranquilizer dart, which he placed in the barrel of the gun. For a moment, I felt like I was watching something on the Animal Channel. He crossed the basketball court, creeping so as to not be detected by the bird. The buzzard's eyes were closed as if he were sleeping. As soon as the barrel of the dart gun rose, four more vultures swooped down and started attacking the animal control officer. They ripped his flesh and screeched. These were twice the size of the one sleeping. Immediately, I grabbed my hand-held radio and called out, "CODE BLUE, REC YARD; CODE BLUE, REC YARD!"

I ran out and glanced back to see Officer Dirk running from the master control booth followed by Captain McBride. My head returned to Peter Miller on the ground now being shredded by the giant vultures. Even though he'd been targeted with the dart, the bird looked unaffected. The animal control officer had crossed his arms in front of his face and eyes, but his belly was exposed, an open season for their claws. With a giant swing of my fist, I punched one off his stomach and grabbed the man's legs. Officer Dirk pushed another off of him and grabbed the man's wrists. By now, the man was motionless as we carried him to the door. Then the son started screaming as Captain McBride grabbed him and began pulling him back inside as we became the next targets for the vultures' deadly claws. At the top of his lungs, Jake cried, "Dad! Help my dad!"

Officer Dirk dropped Peter's legs the moment we entered the facility door. Quickly thinking, I grabbed the fire extinguisher off the wall and sprayed the birds as they tried to follow us in before Captain McBride locked the door.

"Dad!" the son pathetically screamed.

"Police, ambulance are on their way!" someone announced. I grabbed the teenager's arm and pulled him down the hall as he resisted. He didn't need to see his father ripped to shreds. No boy should.

"Aren't you going to try CPR?" the boy begged. Captain McBride opened the master control side door and motioned me toward the front doors. Around the corner, Jake would not be able to see Officer Dirk trying to hold in his father's belly organs.

"What happened to you?" Captain McBride questioned me. "Are you hurt, too?" I glanced down and realized I was also covered in blood. Quickly, I wiped the blood and checked to make sure I wasn't cut.

"I'm fine. Not my blood."

"You have to save my dad," the boy cried, with his throat almost too tight to speak. Officer Dirk rounded the corner after us, but I didn't need to ask to know that Peter Miller didn't make it. The horror was written across Officer Dirk's ghostly pale face.

"You okay?" I asked him.

"Yeah, you?"

In the distance, I could hear the police and ambulance sirens blaring as they approached. This time, too late.

CHAPTER 8

he water felt good on my skin, coolness running down my body and washing away the blood. I was glad that I kept an extra uniform in my locker. For several minutes I stayed underneath the stream, not wanting to think about what I had just witnessed, the death of an animal control officer. The facility was on lockdown, which meant all the juveniles had to stay in their cells; school and counseling sessions were closed, and none of the officers could go home until lockdown had been cancelled. The cleaning staff was removing the blood, and Officer Dirk had already been interviewed by the detectives. It all seemed like a nightmare. Finally, I redressed into a clean uniform and stared at myself in the mirror. I really didn't want to make this phone call. My husband, although I love him dearly, is a sensitive man, and what I was about to tell him had to be done in a delicate manner. From my locker, I pulled out my cell phone and rang our home number. He answered immediately.

"Hi, honey! How's work going?" he asked. "I already put some beef stew in the Crockpot, so it will be ready for you after my shift at the restaurant." For a moment, I pictured him without his shirt on. His muscles gleaming as he stirred the crock pot.

"We're on lockdown for at least the next twenty-four hours, so I won't be home. Save me a bowl for tomorrow," I hastened to add.

"Lockdown, huh? Mack already causing problems?"

"Some wild animal problem on the property; don't worry about it. I'm safe inside. Mack and all the kids are fine."

"Then why do you have to stay?" He gulped, the roughness in his voice soothed out.

"The state requested some extra security while animal control officers remove the problem. That's all. I'll be inside, so I won't be in any danger at all, honey."

"What is the problem? A black bear?"

"No."

"Panther?" he questioned. "Not a cat."

"It isn't one of those birds like last night, is it?" He gasped, his fearful words echoing of the walls. I hid the truth.

"There's nothing for you to even worry about. I'm kind of pissed I have to stay."

"Was anyone hurt?"

"I'm inside the facility, so there is really nothing for you to worry about, honey," I repeated through gritted teeth.

"What aren't you telling me?" he asked. "What's going on? What happened?" I know the only way out of the questions was to avoid answering so he wouldn't spend the night worrying about my safety, especially after what had happened to our patio door.

"Captain McBride requested more security around the facility because of an animal sighting, and with Jack the Mack around, you know how we need to protect him since he's a boxing superstar."

"What kind of animal?" Officer Dirk poked his head into almost the ladies' shower.

"You dressed, Camp?" I lowered the cell phone.

"Well, if I wasn't, you'd be seeing a lot of skin right now, wouldn't you?"

"Captain McBride is holding a meeting for all of us in her office now. Only skeleton crew on the kids," he continued.

"I'll be right there," I agreed, staying focused on my duty seemed like a Herculean effort. Officer Dirk closed the door, and I raised the cell phone back to my ear. It was then that I noticed that my hand was actually shaking.

"I've got to go."

"Are you okay?"

"Yes! I'll be home in the morning. I'll call you on my breaks until midnight."

"Call me!" he begged.

"Bye." I hung up before he could ask again. I didn't want him to know too much. Outside the shower room, Officer Dirk was waiting for me. We walked tighter down the hallway, made a quick left, and then took a few more steps to the office on the right. Then suddenly he stopped me by a quick grab to the shoulder.

"You tell Louigi what happened?"

"You know I don't give specifics." The color drained from my face.

"It might make the news since there was a death. It would probably be better you tell him, so he doesn't get worried." His frown deepened. Quickly, I faced him.

"You think telling him that a vulture killed a person here is somehow going to make him feel better?"

"If you don't tell him, he might get his news from the news, and we all know what can happen then."

"Panic." I gasped.

"Every parent of these kids will be down here."

"The ones that actually give a crap," I reminded.

"So, a few of them at least."

"So, you've noticed that a lot of these kids don't have parents that care? I noticed that, too, that very few of them even visit." Officer Dirk winced.

"Guess they gave up on them."

"I don't know, but you have a point. Who knows how the news might spin this, and I don't want Louigi to worry more than he already has to."

"He is working today at the restaurant?"

"Yeah. You know that was his dream to own a restaurant. Ever since he was a little boy, he loved cooking. His mother was a famous cook in Italy. She made everything from scratch, and he knew that if he brought her recipes to America, it would really be a hit."

"So that's how he got so good at making that sauce."

"Gravy," I corrected.

"It's called the gravy. Don't ask me. Must be an Italian way of calling pasta sauce."

"Meeting, ten minutes," we heard Captain McBride say from her office. The many voices of others could be heard as well.

"Ten minutes."

"We got ten." Officer Dirk smiled, his crush on the captain was mammoth and hard to hide.

"You want a drink?"

"No, I'm good."

"That was really something."

"I feel bad for that kid," I said. "It's not an easy thing to live without a father. Both Louigi and I grew up without them."

"I didn't know about Louigi. What happened to him?"

"He died not long before he and his mother came to the States. We met at an Italian festival in Vero Beach."

"The one that huge church hosts every year. That one?"

"Yes, that's it. They had this band there. To be honest, they kinda weren't that good, but the singer was good. He sounded a little like Frank Sinatra."

"I love Frank," Officer Dirk admitted.

"My mom would play his records. Which song?"

"He started singing 'It Had to be You,' and Mom just grabbed my hand and dragged me out to the dance floor."

"Isn't that outside?"

"Yeah, it was beside the band's tent underneath string lights and a lot of red, white, and green flags. Everyone was dancing and swaying. She grabbed me and started swaying in the middle of the floor singing the words in a very out-of-tune kind of way."

"Embarrassing?"

"Like you wouldn't believe. My mother loves Frank Sinatra, and she had drunk a lot of wine that night and ate way too much pasta."

"It sounds like a fun night."

"It was now that I think of it. I must have really been turning red, because Louigi came up to me and tapped me on the shoulder and asked me for a dance."

"Romantic."

"When I turned around and saw who asked, I couldn't believe he wanted to dance with me. He was dressed to the nines that night. A pin-striped suit and his hair was slicked back. I'd never seen a man so handsome as he."

"So, you said yes, and the rest was history?"

"Not exactly, right then my mother dropped onto her butt, drunk. I worried she might have hurt herself, so I rushed over to her and helped her back to her feet. She wasn't hurt at all; in fact, she just keeps singing out of tune." Officer Dirk laughed.

"So, did you dance after that?"

"Not exactly. Louigi soon followed me and aided my mom back to her feet. It was then I knew not only was he very handsome but also cared enough about my mother to help her up. I knew he was a winner. Right then, I remember, I thought what a great husband he would make."

"So, love at first sight?"

"You know it, kinda was. But our first meeting was far from all glitter and gold."

"No gold at an Italian festival?" Officer Dirk laughed.

"Okay, there were lots of big necklaces. That's not my point. What happened next should have sent Louigi on his way for good. My mother thanked him for helping her up, and she saw how handsome he was. She gave me a look like 'Wow' and then vomited all over him."

"No way!"

"Yes, way. My very drunk mother puked all over Louigi's expensive three-piece suit. Everyone around us gasped, and the band even stopped playing. It was like everyone in the festival stopped to see the spectacle."

"What did Louigi do?"

"I expected him to be upset. Hell, if it had been my father, he would have slapped her and called her names. But Louigi, not him. He smiled at her and said something like he never liked monkey suits anyways. He smiled at me. He actually smiled and then helped her into a chair nearby. The band started playing, and then he excused himself to go to the bathroom to wash up. I was never so embarrassed in my life. I didn't think he would come back, but about fifteen minutes later he came back and sat down next to us. He had removed his jacket and had even changed shirts. When 'My Way' started, that was it. He grabbed my hand and took me back out onto the floor while my mother slept with her head on the table. She never did see the greatest moment of my life."

"You all gonna join us?" Captain McBride called us into her office. The room was filled with corrections officers surrounding Ms. McBride's large mahogany desk. She was leaned back, clicking her pen as we came in. "About time," she said.

"Sorry, we were talking," I explained. Captain McBride rose to her feet and started the meeting. Finally, she stopped clicking her pen.

CHAPTER 9

"We've had a death this morning caused by some wild vultures. Animal control is sending special reinforcements from Orlando which should arrive in about an hour," Ms. McBride said, struggling to keep her shaking hands still.

"They need to bring me a rifle, and I'll take care of them all," Officer Dirk countered with the wariness leaving his face and with a courageous attitude.

"We all know how well you shoot." I smiled, remembering how much time my partner had spent at the gun range. Officer Dirk was the best shooter at the police academy, other than me.

"That sounds like a good idea to me," Officer Dirk said.

"However, vultures are protected Florida wildlife. The actions that they are currently displaying do not fall under their normal behavior patterns. Vultures aren't known for killing anything; they eat mainly roadkill. They eat any dead animal except those that are diseased or have rabies. Animal control would like to capture one for testing to see if we are dealing with some sort of unusual bird disease or even possibly something that could pass to humans."

"Like the Bird Flu or that H1N1 flu did?" Officer Dirk questioned.

"We certainly want to stop or eradicate anything that could spread an illness to the human populations. Our facility is about five miles from the nearest city, so it's good that the majority of the sick birds seem to be congregating here," Captain McBride said.

"Or they tasted blood and want more," I added, "ours."

"Any more good news, Cap?" Officer Dirk questioned, his eyes softening.

"We will remain on lockdown until the situation outside is resolved or the birds fly off. Animal and Florida wildlife officers are actually hoping the birds stay close so they can observe their behavior and capture a few for testing. Right now, we see about a dozen on the light posts, a few on the fence, and about twenty on a nearby dead pine tree. All the birds are so close to the recreation yard that no one, not even personnel, is allowed outdoors without being accompanied by wildlife or an animal control officer. Do I make myself clear?" Captain McBride repeated with the hint of authority in her eyes.

"What about Jack the Mack? He was scheduled to stand before the judge today to see if he will be tried as an adult," Officer Dirk wondered with an inquisitive gaze.

"We know that he is a high-profile case. However, we have alerted the court of our situation and reported that Jack the Mack cannot appear in court today."

"Oh, his lawyer will love that. You know he was going to get him off or have him out on bond so that he could go to the championship boxing match on Friday. That match could make Jack the Mack a national champion boxer," Officer Dirk added.

"The court is aware of the situation," Captain McBride repeated, locking gazes with Officer Dirk. "That is all the responsibility I have on his case. Our job is to keep these kids out of harm's way. We don't listen to the rumors that he's really the devil's spawn."

"That match is his career on the line," Officer Dirk responded, taking a step back and cocking his head. "I don't even watch boxing all that much, but I've seen the advertisements on television, and there was even a clip on TMZ about Jack the Mack getting arrested. This could be perceived a way of keeping him away from his match."

"He took that Rolls Royce. He made it his so we all have to accept that no lawyer can get him off completely from that charge anyway," Captain McBride reminded with a bemused smile. "People pay for their crimes in this state, even if they are celebrities."

"Has anyone told him yet?" I wondered while dozens of scenarios played in my mind.

"You mean the kid himself?" Captain McBride said. "None of the juveniles are aware of the situation that happened with the animal control officer. The press, no one knows; all they know is that we are on lockdown, and no one is allowed within a thousand feet of the facility."

"I'll tell him," I volunteered.

"I'm not sure he deserves the truth."

"He worked hard for that belt. He needs to know that he might not make it to that match. I want the pleasure of telling him myself," I added with a caring tone.

"He's a good kid with a criminal father," another officer said.

"Be gentle."

"Really? Good kids don't break the law in my book."

"All right," Captain McBride said.

"You tell Jack the Mack that he isn't going to trial today so he can call his lawyer and let him know. The last thing we need is a lawsuit over the lawyer's time because he went to trial when Jack the Mack couldn't show up."

"Okay," I agreed.

"But do…do it gently," Captain McBride said with a sweet, caring smile. "I don't want a fight or have to put him in confinement over this. It's bad enough we've had a death in the facility."

"I will. I think we should also tell the kids why they are on lockdown. We can mention wild animal loose outside without telling them someone died. That way they won't request time in the yard." Captain McBride agreed with a smile.

"Good thinking. Whatever makes this easier on everyone involved. I don't think we'll be long in lockdown. Animal officers should be able to control the vultures, and then we can return to normal shifts."

"I got a hot date tomorrow night," a male officer said. "I don't want to miss it over some stupid birds."

"Actually, vultures are not dumb," in walks another Wildlife Officer wearing an Indiana Jones-type hat and a brown uniform with a Florida Wildlife badge on the left breast.

"Can we help you?" Captain McBride asked.

"My name is Rudy Chance. Chance for short. I'm going to capture the birds, all of them, stick them in my cages, and you all will be going outside in about three hours."

"Really?" I smiled. "That's what the last guy said. He said fifteen minutes, and he winded up in pieces." Chance tapped his cowboy hat.

"He wasn't a Florida cracker who'd been raised among these big black beauties." He was cocky and fearless. Of that there was no question. Men like that have to be, I guessed. It would take fearlessness, but unfortunately, Chance reminded me too much of Peter Miller, the first man who just left a boy fatherless.

"Welcome." Captain McBride stood and shook his hand.

"All of us are here to help."

It was then I remembered it was Sunday, and my mom, Lucinda, always went to the beach late Sunday afternoon to layout and collect seashells. Immediately, I rushed out of the room to make a quick call.

My mom's phone just rang and rang. I wanted to warn her about the vultures. Who knows how far they might have traveled? The public did need to be warned as soon as possible that there was danger in the skies above.

CHAPTER 10

THERE'S BLOOD IN THE WATER.

While Lucinda swam twenty feet from the shoreline, she tried not to panic. Florida beaches are known for many things: beautiful sand, lots of shells, and sharks near Sebastian Inlet. The smell of blood invaded in her nostrils. Whatever was bleeding was bleeding badly and nearby. Suddenly, Lucinda saw a dark, greyish-black fin break the surface moving rapidly about ten feet away. "Shark!" She heard a cry from the dunes. Lucinda glanced to shore to see a young, teenage surfer with platinum hair waving his arms for her to come back to land. A seagull scolded her overhead.

"Shark, lady! Get out of the water! Now!"

She didn't have time to see that the monster-size shark had turned in her direction because she encountered something else in the water. Her eyes focused down on the giant swordfish that had been bitten in half. Running into the shark's prey made her swim even faster. Her arms began doing the breaststroke at a speed she had never achieved before. In a few very long seconds, Lucinda reached the shore and ran toward the young man with the longboard at his feet.

"Yo, that was a close call!" he sympathized. Lucinda whirled around to see the shark raise up his giant jaw just enough to engulf the rest of the marlin's head, biting though the skull so only the sword of the fish remained.

"That's a great white motherfucker!" She inhaled deeply, trying to catch her breath. She wanted to ask him if he kissed his mother with that dirty mouth, but he was too cute. Brilliant blue eyes, long blonde hair, and a dark suntan framed his well-defined physique. In fact, his dark skin proved he practically lived on the beach. He even looked a little like surfer Kelly Slater in the face.

"I made it," Lucinda sputtered.

"By the skin of your chinny-chin-chin, ya did. We probably shouldn't be out here anyway. Did you hear about the vultures going crazy at that juvie jail and killing somebody?" She grabbed her towel off the beach sand and began drying off.

"In Cocoa? My daughter works there."

"Not sure. Maybe up north. Heard vultures are killing people, like Hitchcock kinda stuff." He picked up his board. "Well, no surfin' today. Watch the skies, too." With that, he sauntered away, and she noticed his tight butt.

"My name's Lucinda," she said. "You want my number?"

He waved back and chuckled. "I told you to watch the skies, not reach for the stars."

"Out of my league?" Lucinda asked.

"Naw, you're righteous for an ol' broad. Just shackled already," he added. A dark spot fluttered over the water. It wasn't a sea gull either. It was very odd to see a giant black vulture circling above the remains of the marlin on the ocean surface, not over inland roadkill. Lucinda picked up her cell phone out of her beach towel.

"He's cute. But crazy. Vultures wouldn't attack humans." Hearing the phone ringing, she immediately picked it up, recognizing the number.

"Mom?"

"Yeah, some guy on the beach just told me somebody was killed at a jail by vultures. Sounds crazy, his talk; then I saw you called."

"It's true. All of it," I admitted to my mother. "We're on lockdown, and an animal control officer is trying to capture one of the vultures to see what disease it has. It's like nothing I've ever seen!"

"There is a vulture circling what's left of a swordfish in the water now!" Lucinda said.

"You need to get inside, Mom."

"Okay." Lucinda began to hurry from the beach to the parking lot.

"Get into your car. Do you still see the vulture? Is it anywhere near you now?" Lucinda looked over to the ocean, and the bird was gone. All that was left was the blood in the water. She glanced around all over the skies.

"Where did he go?"

"So he's gone?"

"It looks that way." Lucinda continued to hurry into the parking lot and weaved in between the cars searching for her sedan. She fumbled for her remote to open her car doors. It was then Lucinda saw the massive black bird swooping down. She screamed, clicked the remote, and got into her car just as the bird dived toward her.

"Mom, what happened?"

"A bird swooped down at me, but I'm okay. I'm in my car now." She locked the door and peered out through her driver's window in search for where the bird had gone.

"I don't know where it is." Wham! Lucinda screamed. The vulture was sitting on her driver's side mirror pecking at her window. It cracked. "It's here. Outside. It's trying to get in!"

"Start the car, Mom. Drive off. It won't be able to keep up." I clutched my phone. "Do it now! Hurry!"

"The window is breaking." Lucinda pressed the start button in her small sedan and went into reverse as fast as she could. The bird tittered and then fell off onto the pavement. There was blood surrounding him around his wing. The fall had injured the bird enough that he couldn't fly. At least, that's what Lucinda thought when she nearly rolled down her window. But the bird sat back up and expanded its wings. Lucinda turned the car and sped away, screeching the tires.

"Mom, are you okay?"

"Yes, I'm on the highway going away from the beach. I'm on my way home now."

"I'll call you later. Stay inside! I've got to go talk to one of the inmates, and I'll call you later."

"Be safe, honey. Love you."

Chapter 11

All the way to Jack's cell I prepared what I was going to say. I didn't really want to tell him he would probably not make it to the championships, but he had the right to know. Officer Dirk came around the corner. He blurted out, "You want back up in case he gets violent." I nodded yes. My smile faltered. As we stood in front of the glass in the door, Jack the Mack, the six-foot-two, seventeen-year-old male, rose from the cement slab to his feet. Even though he was large, he looked no different than many of the teenage boys that we have kept in the facility before; the only difference was the muscles.

"I am ready to vamoose. You guys coming to take me to court?" was his first question.

"Sit down; hands where we can see them."

"Awe naw." He grimaced.

"Sit down; and put your hands where we can see them."

"I've done nothing wrong," Jack protested. The displeasure glimmered in his eyes. "I told you guys that I am innocent. It's the truth!"

"Yeah, we've never heard that one before." Officer Dirk smirked and slanted a grin my way.

"Sit down and put your hands where we can see them," I repeated.

"My lawyer will get me out of this before Friday."

"Don't make me sit you down," Officer Dirk warned. Jack took one step toward me, and that was all the warning Officer Dirk needed to slam his hand on the top of Jack's shoulder and push him down to sit back on the cement slab.

"You really going to play me like this." Jack gasped.

"Put your hands where we can see them," I ordered. The bleakness on his face surprisingly pained me. Slowly, he raised both hands and put one hand on each knee. Officer Dirk still had a grasp on his shoulder.

"Do you guys realize what I have going on Friday? I'm going to become the next heavyweight champion in my division," Jack announced. "I've got to get before the judge and get out of here."

"I wish I had better news for you," I said standing above him. The words lodged in my heart. "Because of a wild animal attack, we are on lockdown until Florida Wildlife officers and animal control can remove the problem. It may take the afternoon, so court was cancelled."

Surprisingly, he laughed.

"You think I'm afraid of some kind of gator or raccoon? Do you know who I am? Do you realize what is at stake here? Are you guys putting me on?" he scoffed. The desperation in his voice tugged at her heart. "It's the national championship!"

"We have to follow state procedures, and I'm afraid that when an outside threat is deemed, the facility remains on lockdown."

"What about my lawyer?"

"You're a minor, so without your lawyer or a parent present to discuss your case, I'm afraid you're up a creek without a paddle," Officer Dirk commented.

"So, what you are telling me is that because of some animal, I can't get my championship belt?"

"No, because you stole a Rolls Royce out of your neighbor's garage and took it for a spin. He reported it stolen, and now you are facing grand theft charges," Officer Dirk snipped, his shoulders tightening like a linebacker's.

"You kids never take responsibility for your own actions. It's always the officer's fault or the lawyer's, not your fault for doing something wrong in the first place." Jack lowered his gaze.

"You're right, dawg. Can I at least call my lawyer or my mom?" I nodded that he could. "Thanks, I appreciate it."

"We'll take you down to the phone and give you fifteen minutes to break the news to your lawyer."

"Officer Camp is very generous. Normally it's only five minutes of time granted," Officer Dirk explained. Jack closed his eyes for a moment.

"I can't believe this. What kind of animal put this whole building on lockdown?" I didn't answer. Officer Dirk slowly removed his hand.

"Walk in front, hands kept behind your back until you get to the phone at the end of the hallway."

"Yes, officer," he mumbled stepping to the bars, waiting to be let out of the cell. When Jack stood, I was again reminded how big this seventeen-year-old kid was, one who might have become a national boxing champion.

CHAPTER 12

As we were walking down the hall, his fellow gang members shouted, "Here comes the champ!"

It made me sad for a brief moment that what had happened could possibly keep him from getting to the ring. I shouldn't have felt that way. I'm supposed to be impartial, but I just couldn't help it. Jack didn't seem to be the monster his reputation made him out to be. I also understood what it was like to have an absent father. He was a criminal and rumored to be extremely abusive to both Jack and his mother who died of cancer. Jack had some hard breaks in life, but he did turn it around to make a boxing career that could set him financially for life, that is, if he ever got there.

"Stop her!" I heard Captain McBride's voice. Around the corner, a woman stood being held back by two corrections officers. She was strikingly beautiful, with small features, bright green eyes, and red hair. Even though she was thin, she was trying to escape her captives.

"Let me go!" Her expression softened, and her big eyes flickered.

"Who the hell are you?" Captain McBride asked her.

"I don't know if you realize this, but this is juvenile jail, and most people don't try to break in here; they try to escape."

"Let this little filly break in," Jack said with a stone expression.

"She's a firecracker."

"I'm not a filly or a firecracker, Mr. Mack. I am a reporter for the *Sun*, and there has been a death at this facility which may stop you from getting to the ring Friday night. The public and your fans have a right to know why and what happened to Peter Miller."

"Awe, crap." Captain McBride shook her head. "That still doesn't give you the right to drive into our garage and pretend to be a food delivery service agent."

"You thought she was food service." Jack laughed. "What's your name, beautiful?" The redhead stopped fighting the officers and straightened out her skirt.

"I'm Darla Matthews, and I work for the *Sun* as a sports reporter."

"You're Darla?" Officer Dirk.

"Yeah, she's on the radio show. I heard her before. She's legit, Cap."

"You may be who you say you are, but you can't just break into my facility and do an interview." She needed to hear it.

"Why not?" Jack asked her.

"It's not visiting hour."

"Do you think reporters go by visiting hours? Do you realize the significance of this young man being behind bars? Proceeds from that match were going to St. Jude."

"St. Jude?" Captain McBride's face showed horror. Her doubt shouldn't have stung, but it did. "Is that true?"

"Yeah, I think so. Funny how your son goes there, and I am trying to raise a million dollars for the hospital. This whole bird thing may even stop me from going."

"You're trying to raise money for St. Jude?" Captain McBride's pupils dilated as she spied Jack's face.

"My mom had cancer," Jack reminded, spinning toward her with a scowl on his face. "She didn't go there but her doctor, Dr. Burton works there. So, I am doing it to help raise money to fight cancer. Their research goes to help everyone, not just kids. I got a sponsor who said if I win, he'll donate the million dollars to the hospital." Captain McBride's eyes welled with tears. Her faith in humanity lifted.

"I didn't know."

"It's part of the story that was to go in the paper along with the news that he's been put here for stealing a car."

"That's got to be in your article?" Jack grimaced.

"Yes, and also your father's gotten permission from the governor to be ringside. Then this death happened here, and the public has a right to know what's going on! Will you be there Friday?" Darla asked, her question chilling him to the bone. Jack glanced over to Captain McBride.

"Well, will I be, Captain?'

"A million dollars for St. Jude's?" she questioned hopefully.

"Yes, ma'am."

"He did steal a car, Cap," Officer Dirk reminded.

"But for the hospital, we should try our best to get him to the ring Friday." "My officers will take you and bring you right back. You've got to get permission from a judge, too." Jack nodded.

"Whatever it takes."

"So, you're going to be there?" Darla questioned Jack.

"I'm gonna try." Captain McBride said, "I can't believe I'm saying this for a car-stealing gang member, but I will do my best to pull a few strings." Jack's eyes lit up.

"Thank you! I'm gonna win!"

"Are you excited that your father will be in attendance?" Darla asked him.

"Actually," Jack was going to say no, and we all knew it. He almost said it and then thought the better of it.

"My dad reads your paper, so I am just going to say that this whole thing is a dream come true. I regret taking that car, too."

"This is a great story!" Darla told Captain McBride.

"We could arrest you," Captain McBride told her.

"You better never do this again, ever! Because next time, I will. This is a locked down facility, and these kids don't have all their rights, which includes freedom of speech."

"I understand," Darla said. "Now, may I go?"

"Don't ever come back here," Captain McBride said authoritatively. "If I ever see that bright red hair again, your body will be in cuffs."

"You don't need to worry. I just needed the information to finish my article. I also need more information about the death. The man left behind a wife and two boys. What exactly happened here?"

"Go ahead," Jack told Captain McBride. "She'll never believe you anyway."

"Give him a call, and Darla, come into my office. This is going to be shocking for you, and we need to handle things not to scare the public." With that, Darla followed the captain into her office, and we went to the phone down the hall.

CHAPTER 13

At the phone, Jack dialed a number; Officer Dirk and I stood a few feet behind him as he spoke to his mother about contacting their family lawyer. He asked if she could have the lawyer change the court date to Friday morning. As long as he could get released sometime in the afternoon, he could make the championship match. I glanced over to the outside door and saw the vultures gathering on the pine tree. Jack must have noticed the big black birds, too, because for a moment he paused and stopped speaking to his mother.

"Three more minutes," I warned; dread curled my stomach. My blood pressure seemed to rise spying the vultures. Jack continued to converse, telling his mother to not come to visit him until the lockdown was over.

"Don't come, Maw," he said. "Something is happening here, and I've got to clear my head." Suddenly, Jack hung up the phone and turned on a heel. A volley of expletives burst out of his mouth.

"Did something out there die? Do you see all them?" he asked us.

"So many buzzards."

"There's nothing for you to be concerned with inside," Officer Dirk said. The wind howled against the barred windows. Jack took a step toward the door, and Officer Dirk immediately warned, "Time to go back to your cell now."

"I just want to take a look, man. The door is locked without a code. What's the matter?" I nodded as pounding started in my ears.

"Take a quick look then." Officer Dirk leaned into me and whispered, "I don't think that's such a good idea."

"Let him see for himself why we are on lockdown. Maybe then he won't be so upset with the whole thing and realize we are just protecting everyone inside."

When he went to the door, Jack's eyes widened, and terror crossed his face. "Noooo!" All of a sudden, Jack kicked the door; in two quick strikes the door flew from its hinges. It happened so fast; I didn't have any time to react. That door was reinforced steel. In all my years as a corrections officer, I have never even seen anyone try to break that giant door down. It was rock solid. Then Jack bolted outside. Officer Dirk started running outside after him. I tried to stop him.

"The vultures! Jack can't get out of the yard with the fence! He'll come back."

"He's our responsibility," Officer Dirk shouted back. When we stood at the entrance, we saw what was happening. Jack was being circled by flying vultures. He was in imminent danger. Below the Florida Game officer lay curled up in the fetal position. The boxer was standing over the fallen officer. With one quick move, he removed his shirt and started swinging it in circles over his head to scare the flying birds away. When one got close, he would whip it with his garment.

"Jack's trying to help him," I realized as my mouth went dry. The Florida Wildlife and Game officer started crawling towards us, with hands outstretched and fear in his eyes. I'd never seen a man so terrified. His tranquilizer gun was on the ground; Jack snatched it.

"Oh shit," I said with my mouth dangling open.

"Call for backup!"

A Code Blue went over the speaker system, and several officers came running around the cell floor hallway. Even the captain rushed from the command center. When they got to the door, several of them followed us to surround Jack swirling his shirt. Officer Dirk was the first to order.

"Drop the gun!"

"I've got to get one," Jack said, turning the gun up towards the sky.

"Drop it!" I screamed with infused confidence. Officer Dirk jumped on Jack's back trying to knock him to the ground and take back the gun. With a big left hook, Jack knocked Officer Dirk from around his back, then quickly refilled the gun and shot it again at the sky. This time, he shot one. A big, black vulture fell from the air; I could hear its bones shattering when its large, winged frame slammed onto the basketball court cement. Jack grabbed it with one hand and ran as fast as he could toward the facility. I helped Officer Dirk back to his feet, and we hurriedly followed Jack and the rest of the officers back inside as the birds began swooping down at us; we continued to duck to avoid their claws. When we got inside, two officers reset the door in place and placed several chairs to force it to stay up. The birds continued to fly at the door, cracking the glass, but the door held shut.

"Thank God!" was the last thing I said as my feet hit the floor.

CHAPTER 14

ack handed me the tranquilizer gun back just as I caught my breath. The Florida Wildlife and Game officer was being treated by our staff nurse. Another ambulance was on its way.

"What should I do with this?" Jack held up the motionless giant black bird as his eyes went wide.

"We should probably do something with this before it wakes up." I grabbed it from him and began walking down the hall.

"I'll handle it," I said as his voice broke my paralysis.

"You're going back outside?" gasped Ms. McBride as I hurried past her. "I didn't authorize that."

As soon as the glass door open, I took one step outside. In one hand was the giant black bird, which I held high above my head to show all the vultures perched high above in a pine tree. All around the parking lot, they sat, watching my every move. Slowly, I took another step toward the wildlife and game officer's big white van.

"I have your back," Officer Dirk mumbled behind me, his anguished voice almost a wail. "If one of them moves, I'll see it first."

Quickly, I glanced back toward the door. Officer Dirk and Jack the Mack were standing there with brooms in their hands, ready to strike. Times like this I wish I wasn't a juvenile officer. There were no guns in the facility; only hand weapons were allowed, and Ms. McBride had a stun gun in her purse. Why didn't I think of that before I stepped out into this hell? That stun gun might have knocked a few off of me. Pondering on that, I took several more steps toward the van. There was eeriness in the air. My heart was pounding as I neared the vehicle. None of the giant birds moved an inch. Just their black, beady eyes stared. I hoped there was a cage in the back of this van big enough to hold the creature in my hand. Slowly, I clicked open one side of the van's back doors. I swung it wide and discovered a big metal cage to the right. Outside the cage was a latch, a simple lock that just snapped close to hold whatever the contents. Not sure if that would hold, I stuffed the bird inside and closed the cage with a pair of my handcuffs. When I turned around, I shut the door. All the birds had moved. They were surrounding me now. Slam! One landed on top of the van, inches from my head. Its face was covered in bloody feathers, slobber, and exuded an unusual odor. Is that what death smells like? As soon as I took a step back, the vulture at my feet hopped back. I continued toward the door, without looking any of them in the eye. It took me nearly a minute, but I finally made it back inside the facility. Gasping, I fell to my knees, grabbing the floor, glad to have made it back inside.

"Looks like you did the game officer's job, too," Officer Dirk said, chewing on his lip.

"How is he?"

"McBride just made the announcement that they can reattach the eye at the hospital. Other than that, he'll live."

"Good!" I caught my breath and stood.

"What the hell is going on?" Jack asked. "Buzzards don't act like that to things that are alive."

"We're not sure why. I'm sure this is a fluke," I said with fake optimism.

"Did you get bit or cut earlier?" He nodded no.

"They got close but not close enough."

"That was very quick thinking," Officer Dirk announced. "You were out there before we even knew what was going on. That game officer probably owes you, his life."

"I thought that they were killing him, and I saw the gun on the ground," he explained. "I did what either of you would have done if you had seen it first."

"I'm sure his family will appreciate what you did," I reiterated as I listened to the inmates' voices and heard the howling of the wind. Jack studied the birds on the ground and in the trees.

"They look diseased," he commented. "Is there some kind of outbreak?"

"We'll let animal control figure that out. I am sure they will," I said; my bone-dry mouth told a different story.

"Right now, you need to go back to your cell."

"Really? I think I deserve some time in the mess hall so I can watch a little television and get a snack."

"Get back to your cell."

Without hesitating again, Jack walked back down the hallway into his cell and slammed the door shut. Officer Dirk and I followed, but we didn't need to. He kept his hands raised high without us asking. In truth, I wouldn't have even mentioned it. Jack had suddenly gained our trust. He may be a thief, but he was basically a very brave young man who just wanted out of here. Jack wasn't about to break the rules to make his sentence any worse. He still wanted to get to the national championships. Deep down, despite his criminal gang history, I really wanted Jack the Mack to get to that boxing match and win. Jack just saved a stranger's life at great risk to his own. He didn't even think twice. Jack would actually make a great officer, I realized in an epiphany moment. I would have told Jack that, but I didn't think he'd listen to me. Heading back to Master Control, Officer Dirk and I turned and walked past the man being treated by EMTs, the hallway where the other wildlife officer had been killed. *This is a day I will never be able to forget.*

CHAPTER 15

A few hours had passed, and I went into the breakroom to get out my lunch. Officer Dirk was already sitting in the corner of the room eating a TV dinner, which was steaming hot.

"You okay?" he asked me. His white teeth flashed a smile.

"I am still in shock."

"About Jack saving a man's life or the birds?"

"Both," I admitted, glancing up to a glad face.

"He's not a lost cause."

"Are any of them? I think most of the time they just need parents that care, drug and alcohol rehab, and a good shrink to talk to." Officer Dirk took another bite of what I realized was pepper steak and rice.

"That a good one?"

"Not bad," he admitted, staring her way.

"I guess not KFC now that we are on lockdown," I said.

"Actually, I'm going to start bringing TV dinners for a while. Every day that will save me four dollars, which I'll put in my piggy bank."

"You need money? Is that why you keep working double shifts?" I questioned, his face twisting into a grim.

"No, trying to help out Captain. I want to build a playground for her son." He shot an incredulous glance my way. I grabbed my lunchbox out of the fridge. It had *Bad Boys for Life* on it with Will Smith on the cover. Always thought he was a handsome man, and I loved his movies with Martin Lawrence. Opening my box, I saw the handwritten note from Louigi. "For my love. Enjoy!" He had given me a big bowl of spaghetti and meatballs. There was enough here to feed an army.

"I will help you out with that," I said.

"That's really sweet of you."

"You have something for Captain, don't you?" Officer Dirk smiled.

"Just helping out a friend."

"I think there's more to it," I said, and his exuberance fell away. They locked eyes and held a connection. "But that's your business. I do think your building her son a playground is wonderful."

"As long as these birds are all gone by the time, I get enough money."

"No kidding," I said, wiping the perspiration from my brow with his words holding no reassurance. "Let me know if you are short, and I'll help out. Louigi can help you build it once it's time."

"Really? He can cook and build?"

I showed him my note. "He's a talented man."

"Guess so." Officer Dirk grimaced.

"I won't ever forget the look on that man's face when the vulture's attacked."

"You want some meatballs? You don't seem to be having trouble eating like me," I admitted. Suddenly, Captain McBride entered the break room. In her hand was a sheet of paper and a bag of potato chips.

"Want these?" she asked Officer Dirk.

"Sure." He smiled. "Thanks, Cap."

Then he leaned over to me, "Don't tell her. It's our little secret."

"No problem."

"Tell me what?" Captain McBride heard.

"How beautiful I think you are," Officer Dirk said.

"If you're buttering me up for more overtime, you don't need to. Looks like we're all in for a while until they figure what's happening to the birds around here."

"Just more time with you, Cap," Officer Dirk winked. She blushed but then quickly changed the subject.

"You two are going to be able to drive Jack to the ring tomorrow. You'll have to leave directly from the garage, but I pulled in a favor from the governor. All I had to do was explain how he just saved a man's life. Jack is going to the ring with you two ringsides."

"That's the right thing, Cap," Officer Dirk said.

"Be ready for anything." Captain McBride put her hand on his shoulder supportively.

✳✳✳

"Someday you are going to wear the belt that was robbed from me," Jack's father said to him when he was a child.

"That Smokey hit me with an uppercut to the jaw, and I was knocked out cold. It was a sucker punch, and the buzzer hadn't even sounded. He stole the opportunity away from me to wear that national championship belt. I don't want the same thing to happen to you. I am going to prepare you for anything and everything. You will wear that belt if it's the last thing I ever do."

"I'll get it, Dad. I've been punching the bag and practicing every day with Uncle Michael."

"Michael is a pussy," he said. "I kicked his ass growing up all the time. We've got to train you to be sharp. It's the brain that wins boxing as much as the fists."

"I am smart."

"Not so smart," Jack's father said.

"I got an A on my math quiz."

"I don't care about your grades," he said. "I want you to be street smart, not book smart. Someday you will run my business, and you've got to be street smart and have eyes in the back of your head."

"I can do it," Jack said in the park. A police officer walked by as they were sitting on a park bench.

"Stay away from pigs," Derrick snipped.

"I like cops," Jack said.

"See what I mean." Derrick waited until the cop went far enough down the walkway and around some trees before he taught his son the ultimate lesson. In a second, after making sure no one was looking in the park, he punched his son with an uppercut to the jaw. Jack was laid slowly down, passed out. Then the father slapped his face to wake him up.

"Ouch." Jack rubbed his jaw. "What was that for?"

"Not being street smart. You need to pay attention, always. Next time, you better duck when my fist comes for that chin."

"Next time?" Jack rubbed his chin.

"All the time, be ready from now on. You've got to be instinctive like a cat and hungry like a dog."

"Like Rocky, Dad."

"Rocky was a pussy, too. I fought the real one, not the actor, and won. It was a sucker punch that made me lose the belt. That won't happen to you. I promise you that."

***

The screams were deafening as Jack stepped into the ring in the sold-out Florida auditorium. He'd been waiting for this match for quite some time. Boxing was something that always came easy for him. His father had taught him how to throw a wicked punch when he was six. Quickly, Jack glanced down and saw his father not far from the right side of the ring. *Wasn't there for Mom and me most of our lives, but tonight he got a free night pass out of the state pen.*

"Jack the Mack! Jack the Mack!" Chants from the crowd made him raise his arms like Rocky Balboa. Smiling, he recalled how he got the nickname; his punches were said to hit like a Mack truck.

Next to the father was a strikingly beautiful young woman with long, curly black hair and a figure to die for. She was a teenager but had the body of a supermodel and looks that made everyone stare.

Slightly leaning forward in a striped jumper, Jack could see that both his father's hands and ankles were shackled. His father surely pulled a few strings in the governor's office to be ringside.

The young woman standing next to his father waved to Jack and blew him a kiss. Jack winked to her, and it was then I realized that must be Jack's girlfriend and not his father's. She was wearing a cling-style dress that was so low cut you could almost see the nipples of her enlarged breasts.

Slowly, his father's eyes raised to his. They locked when Jack looked away from the young woman to his father's face.

"Take him out," his father mouthed. Jack's opponent walked into the ring, not quite as tall but about the same muscular build. Only one big difference: his enemy was from a rival gang, and if Jack didn't knock him out, his face would be the one hitting the mat. His enemy looked a little scared, shaking a bit. The two boxers met in the middle, knocked gloves, and then the referee quickly pointed to the side. The bell rung.

The match started. Jack took two steps back. He gave his first upper-cut punch to the jaw with all the strength that he musters. The strike hit just like his nickname, like a Mack truck. In less than two seconds, his rival Johnny was down. The crowd jumped to its feet. The hoots and hollers were so loud they hurt Mack's ears. By the ropes, Johnny lay motionless. His crew rushing to his side.

"Jack the Mack! Jack the Mack!" chanted the crowd. *Did what you wanted, Dad.* Mack glanced one last time at his smiling father. Jack heard the referee tell Johnny's coach, "He's out cold."

Jack grinned down as his father was led out of the auditorium in handcuffs by six corrections officers from the state pen. Officer Camp and Dirk then motioned for him to step down from the ring to return to juvenile jail.

CHAPTER 16

I watched him like a hawk, but Jack stepped down from the ring, not a scratch on him from the opponent, and raised his hands to be cuffed.

"We'll do that in the van," Officer Dirk said, then looked at me for approval. I shook my head yes. Jack hadn't given us one bit of trouble this entire trip. Of course, he didn't want trouble to stop the match. For good reason. He's now won the national championship belt. At seventeen, his career was made for him. He has a golden ticket to a good life, yet I couldn't help but feel sorry for him. His father owned him. At least, that's how it seems. At seventeen, he was doing whatever his father and the Union gang wanted him to do. He may be the champion of the world, but he wasn't living the life he had chosen but what others had chosen for him. We walked through the screaming crowd when suddenly the young woman who had been standing next to his father came up behind us and yelled, "Jack!"

Jack stopped and turned around. The look on his face when he saw her told the story of his love for her. His arms opened and in flew the brunette.

"Hello, Marla," he greeted and caught her in a fierce embrace, then turned to us. "This is my girl, Marla."

"Hands off, Marla," Officer Dirk pulled her out of his arms.

"Oh, it's like that," Jack said, disappointedly.

"No contact." Officer Dirk nodded. "Now, go."

"I love you, baby," she said. "I am so proud of you."

"Pops taking good care of you?" he asked her.

"Yes." Marla went to hug him again, but Officer Dirk pulled her back.

"No contact, miss."

"Her name's Marla." Jack winked to her again. "And I am going to marry her one day."

"I love you," she said with an adamant expression.

"Behave yourself, Marla. I'll be out in no time at all," Jack said, then turned around and continued to walk through the crowd toward the tunnel. Everyone's hands out were for him to pat or shake as we went by. Then he got to the tunnel. Jack suddenly stopped and turned around to face us. As soon as the tunnel door shut and we could hear him through the screams of joy, he spoke.

"Thank you so much," he said to Officer Dirk. "This was awesome of you all to make sure I got here and was able to win the belt. I won't forget this. I even got to see my girl for a minute."

"We won't forget how you saved a life," Officer Dirk said.

"Yes, that was much braver than what you just did," I added with my pulse speeding up with the thoughts of the death.

"This was nothing." Jack chuckled. "My father is an asshole, but he made sure I would be ready to win."

"So, the children's hospital will get that money now?" I asked.

"Yes, it was a donor who offered to put up the money; that didn't come from me or the Union."

"Good motivation," I said.

"Actually, I learned either way this donor would have given. It was all hype for the press. They love a good story. Whatever sells. Didn't you see how they kept taking shots of my Dad? Having a con as a father is a story, too, but they don't know what he's like. My pops is deadly. His lawyer said all the evidence was circumstantial, but my pops is a killer. He still leads the Union and the boxing joint all from jail."

"Well, you are not him," I said. "I saw something in you when you went to protect that animal control officer." Jack just shook his shoulders and started walking down the tunnel towards the parking lot. Once we got to the door, we could hear screaming outside.

"Wait here," Officer Dirk said. "I'll go get the van."

"What's going on?" I peered through the glass doorway and saw a vulture swooping down at the crowd leaving the area. People began running for their cars. Just then, I saw a security guard take out a taser and shoot it down to the ground. Being shocked, it was shaking on the ground.

"They are out here, too." Jack seemed surprised.

"We're an hour away from the facility." I gasped. Panic threatened to overtake me, but I pushed it back. My adrenaline spiked. The transportation van drove right up to the door going over the grass.

"Get in," Officer Dirk shouted. His hands trembled as he looked out the window at Jack. Jack rushed out the door looking up at the skies, but there were no more birds in sight. He flipped open the side door, got in, and sat in the seat. I shut the door and hopped into the passenger's door. I knew I should have put him in cuffs before he got in, but I didn't think of it. My mind was too busy looking up in fear of the birds.

"You didn't handcuff him," Officer Dirk reminded me as he zipped up his jacket.

"We're good," I said and exhaled.

"He'll cause us no trouble." Jack sat back in his seat looking at me, surprised. Officer Dirk started the van down the highway toward the juvenile jail. I could tell he wasn't happy that I hadn't cuffed Jack. His eyes were peering through the bars at Jack, glancing back and forth from the road back to Jack who was just sitting in his seat. Jack seemed calm. Not like someone who had just won one of the greatest honors in sports today.

"Something's up." I sensed as my brow lifted, and a frown curled my face. Officer Dirk agreed with me.

"Something is up. He's just sitting there like he's waiting for something."

"I should have cuffed him."

"You think we're being paranoid?"

Officer Dirk reached over for the taser gun in the glove box. Jack smiled then, not to us, but back toward a semi-truck who was speeding coming our way. "Oh, shit," Officer Dirk said with a scowl. Before we knew it, the semi-truck was alongside the van. It had a teenager with a gun pointed right at my head.

"Pull over," the kid said.

"This is bulletproof glass," Officer Dirk reminded as he hit the gas pedal.

"I'll outrun him."

It was then the semi hit our van, which caused the van to flip onto its side. The hit sideways made my head hit the door, and all I saw was blood pouring down my forehead. A hand touched my shoulder.

"You okay? Get the taser gun," Officer Dirk pointed to in front of me, but I couldn't seem to move. I'd never seen Officer Dirk so rattled. Someone tried to open my door, but it was locked. Another man put something on the side door. The explosion caused my ears to ring, and that's when I saw them pull Jack out of the van. They carried him because he was out cold, so they carried him to the back of the semi and tossed him in like a rag doll. I was hoping they would just leave us behind; I prayed for a moment then that they would. No luck. One more door explosion, and my door flung open. Arms reached in and grabbed Officer Dirk and me. I couldn't fight back as they dragged me and threw me into the back of the semi, but Officer Dirk did. Three of them surrounded him, and he gave a fight. He punched a few times, but one had a bat and hit him in the stomach. He fell onto the ground, and then the bat hit him on the head. He didn't move after that. Instead, they picked up his motionless body and tossed him in to lie beside me. I couldn't see their faces well as they shut the door. But I did feel him gently push away the hair in my face.

"You okay, Officer Camp?" I recognized Jack's voice. Officer Dirk slowly rolled over onto his back and grabbed his head.

"That hurt."

Jack wiped the blood off of my face with the end of his shirt. "You okay, Camp?"

"What about me?" Officer Dirk sat up. "I am a little damaged."

"Sorry," Jack said. "I didn't know that my boys were coming for me, and I sure didn't tell them to hurt you both."

Now that I could see. My head hurt, but I realized I had been nearly knocked out, but I was alive. At least, I was so far. "Your boys are going to kill us since we know who they are," I realized, struggling to maintain my equilibrium.

"Not on my watch," Jack said.

"All you had to do was go back to the facility," I reminded. "You would have probably gotten less than six months for stealing that car. Now you've got jail break on your record. This is not going to help you."

"No kidding." Jack made sure all the blood was away from my eyes and then rolled down the tip of his shirt, which was now covered in blood. The truck started moving. The light from the tiny black window was hardly sufficient for me to see my surroundings. It appeared the semi was empty except for the three of us and the three who had kidnapped us sitting in the cab.

"You got to believe me," Jack said. "I saw the truck coming, but I thought they were coming to cheer me on, not kidnap us."

"So you don't know where we are going?" Officer Dirk padded his head. "Great, I'm going to have a huge bump on my head."

"Better a bump than dead," I said. "I don't think I am strong enough to fight them off right now."

"You lost a lot of blood," Jack said. "It looks like you'll live, though."

"I wouldn't count on that," Officer Dirk said.

"We know who they are. They aren't going to let us live. What is your best guess where they are taking us?"

"Headquarters would be my thought, which is the Union Boxing House, but that might be the first place the cops would look for me, so I don't know really. I honestly didn't know this was going to happen."

"Are you surprised?" I asked.

"Truth be told, no. You don't mess with the Union and their peeps. I am not surprised, but I am a little pissed. I was hoping my lawyer could get me out of this mess now that I raised all that money for the hospital. Now they've ruined my chances."

We were all silent for a few minutes. Officer Dirk was patting his head, and I leaned over and looked at the big bump on the side of his head. "You might have a concussion."

"You think?" he said sarcastically. Suddenly, the door opened, and the three of the young men were standing in a row with guns.

"Get out," the one in the middle said. We did as we were told. They gave Jack fist bumps as he passed them. We were in the driveway of what looked like a very old farm. I guessed we weren't far from the arena but in West Melbourne somewhere near the horse ranches. For miles there was nothing but grass and the farmhouse in front of us. An old-fashioned barn looked to be about a half mile away on the expansive property.

"This is my uncle's ranch," Jack told us.

"Your pops is inside," the third one told Jack.

"You got him out, too?" Jack gasped. He nodded yes and pointed to the door. Officer Dirk and I trailed behind Jack as the men with guns followed us. Having guns pointed at my back by three Union gang members did not feel good. The ground seems to spin a little. No, I wasn't well. I'd like to think that it was only blood loss, but I honestly wasn't sure of my condition. Jack opened the door, and we all walked inside to what looked like a living room next to a giant kitchen. It was ranch style, with bull's horns above the fireplace and items that looked like they would be better displayed in a barn.

"Greetings," said a man standing next to Jack's father. I recognized him at least from the championship match.

"Pops." Jack went up to his father, and his father embraced him.

"I should have let you know that this was going to go down tonight, but I got word that we could be moved to Mexico City. We've got members there willing to bring us in and take care of things." Jack shook his head.

"Pops, I gotta go back to juvie."

"The vultures!" His father gasped. "No, we are moving to Mexico. I already had your things packed up. We are going tonight, and as far as the USA is concerned, we disappeared tonight after you became world champion."

"And what about us?" Officer Dirk said, then he moved to the right. That's when I saw six other officers hog tied in the kitchen with gags in their mouths. I surmised that they were the officers that had been transporting Jack's father.

"What are you going to do to us?" Jack's father took a step closer to us and then took a deep breath.

"You'll all die."

CHAPTER 17

"Now, let's talk about this." Officer Dirk raised his hand. His eyes grew luminous. "There's no need to kill any of us. Just go."

"Pops, there's no reason to kill anybody."

"We don't need any witnesses to this, Jack. The jet leaves in thirty minutes. All of our things are being sent in trucks as we speak. In a few hours, we'll start a new life. The both of us. Neither of us needs to ever be in a cell again."

"I hear ya," Jack said. Anger darkened his voice. "But this isn't going to make our crimes go away."

"We can disappear in Mexico and live like kings," promised Jack's father Derrek. The man standing next to Jack's father suddenly spoke,

"My name is Michael, and I am Jack's uncle, Derrek's brother."

"I'm Laura," I said. My back prickled with gooseflesh.

"You've got a nasty cut on your head, Laura." Michael touched my scalp and moved my hair so he could get a better look. "Would you like me to sew that up for you?"

"We're going to kill her," Derrek said. The dark circles under his eyes emphasized his stress.

"Why would you do that?"

One of the gang members stepped forward, raising the gun, "Say the word, and it's done."

"Stop it," Jack raised his voice. His intense eyes willed his father to listen. "Stop threatening a cop."

"Corrections officer," I corrected Jack. "I am not going to arrest anybody. I just want to go back to the Juvie. It's surrounded by bloodthirsty vultures at the moment, and it is my job to make sure everyone's safe."

"Just let us go," Officer Dirk said with a defiant tilt in his chin.

"Let all of us go."

"I don't have much of a choice in the matter." Jack's father touched the shoulder of his son.

"Jack is world champion now. The world knows who he is. He's made me the proudest father on Earth. But now it has come time for us to leave America behind and start a life where we both can live free."

"You won't be free," I said. My eyes widened with terror. "You kill us, and every cop will be after you for the rest of your life. That kind of crime doesn't go unnoticed anywhere, not even in Mexico."

"The Union has power there," Derrek said. "No one will be able to stop us there. We have places we can hide and still live like kings."

"Is running living like a king, Jack?" My voice choked. Jack shook his head with a jerky nod.

"Pops, I didn't want this. I got a lawyer coming to get me off from stealing that car. I don't want a life on the run."

"That isn't a choice now!" Derrek roared. "I did all this for you."

Suddenly, the door opened, and in walked a young Latina woman wearing a skin-tight dress.

"Jack," she breathed as her long-nailed hands wrapped around his thick neck, and her bright red lips rose to kiss his. "I missed you so much."

"Marla." Jack smiled. "Hello, baby."

"In the flesh," she said. "I love you."

Jack kissed her again with a smack of the lips. "Did you know about my dad breaking me out and wanting me to move to Mexico?"

"Yes, baby," she said. "We could have a new life together. I've missed you so much!"

I realized then that saving Jack from ruining his life was never going to happen. He obviously was in love with this very beautiful young woman. Marla flipped her long, curly black hair and then kissed Jack quickly on the cheek.

"We need to do what pops want," Marla said, shrinking back.

"You're in on this." Jack pushed her away. "Without even talking to me about it? Did it ever occur to you that I am happy in America? I'm like the next Rocky, and I've got to stay in the ring."

"That life you can live in Mexico," Derrek said.

"Maybe he has a point, brother." Uncle Michael nodded. "The boy doesn't need to go with you. You could go."

"I'd never see him again," Derrek reminded. "I am building a bigger Union there where we will have no Crowns to fight us. We'll rule the gambling halls."

"Is that what you want?" I asked Jack.

"To live the life of a gangster, forever? You are a good person."

"Shut up," Derrek said, waving his gun. "You don't know my boy."

"This is his Darth Vader moment," I said. "I had the same type of moment when my mother nearly killed my father. I had to decide at that moment if I wanted my father to live or die. I no longer wanted him to control my life and destroy the life of my mother and me. I decided in a single moment that I wanted to do the right thing."

"What is your right thing?" Officer Dirk faced Jack. "Is it killing officers and living a life of crime for your father or making the choice to come back with us to Juvie where you can do things the right way and get your life back on your own terms?"

"Son, why are you even listening to these pigs?" Jack faced him.

"Don't call them that."

I half hoped that he was going to walk away with us.

"I am calling them what they are! They are nothing but pigs that try to stop us from living our lives."

"They are just doing their job," Jack said. "They risked their lives to help save a man today from vultures."

"You did that, too," I reminded him.

"I did, Pops. I saved a man today," Jack told him. "You didn't even know that. All you care about is running and doing more crimes. What if I want more from my life than that? What if I want a real life for Marla and me?"

"We have no life away from the Union. The Crowns will kill us," Marla reminded. "Your father protects us!" She poked his arm.

"You're dead wrong," I said. "He's leading down a road where you won't be able to return, Jack. He's leading you down the wrong path, and it will only get you killed in Mexico, and you'll have to look over your shoulder for the rest of your life."

Chapter 18

It was then that the room started swimming. My eyes rolled back, and my legs went limp. Before my body fainted, Officer Dirk grabbed me and carried me to a nearby bedroom. I expected the gang members to stop him, but they didn't. Jack was following us as he laid me down on top of the bed.

"She's lost too much blood," Jack said. His hooded eyes wouldn't meet my gaze.

"We need to get Camp to a hospital," Officer Dirk shuddered.

"She's pale," Jack commented, raising a pillow to sit behind my head. I had to admit, lying down was helping.

"You shouldn't care," Derrek snipped. "She's nothing but a pig."

"Stop it!" Jack said shoving his hands into his pockets. "These two brought me to a new cell so I wouldn't be killed by the Crowns. They protected me, Pops!"

Suddenly, Derrek's demeanor changed. His angry expression turned to compassion. "They helped you?"

"Yeah, Pops. The captain even has a kid at St. Jude's. It wasn't great, but they helped me while I was in there. I wouldn't have gone to the ring if it wasn't for these people doing what they could for me. They didn't have to do that. I took that car, Pops. They were just doing their jobs, and they don't deserve to die just because you want us to move to Mexico."

"Let me talk to him." Marla touched Derrek's arm, and she forced a smile. Derrek nodded and waved for everyone else to leave the bedroom. Marla and Jack sat down next to me on the bed. Officer Dirk kneeled down next to me not about to leave my side in the room.

"Ten minutes." Derrek then shut the door. When he did, I realized Marla and Jack were distracted. I grabbed my pants and raised it just so my right leg would show my ankle. Officer Dirk saw the tracking device snapped onto my shoe and suddenly smiled.

"They'll know," he whispered. I quickly pushed my pant leg down as Marla wrapped her arms around Jack's neck and gave him another kiss.

"I think we should go to Mexico."

"I'm not going," Jack told her with a serious expression.

"I want us to go so you won't be in jail no more." Marla pouted with pursed, full lips.

"I did the crime, so I'll do the time," Jack said with color returning to his cheeks.

"But I'm going crazy without you. I can't do this. The Crowns are relentless, and they want to take over the city. In Mexico, your uncle owns an underground casino. Michael will set us up, and the Union will be reborn." He stroked his arm.

"You'd live like a queen then." Jack thought it over.

"More like the princess to my prince." Marla stroked his hair gently. "I love you, baby."

"I know," Jack said. "But I am already a prince in this town."

"One that the Crowns wants dead," she reminded.

"Then we're nothing but cowards on the run," Jack said. He kissed her again. "I need more than that. I want us to get married."

I looked at him for a moment. This very strong young man did seem to be head over heels for her, and who wouldn't be? Marla was absolutely strikingly beautiful. Even Officer Dirk, who was in love with McBride, couldn't take his eyes off of her. When he kissed her again, the back of his arm slightly lifted her shirt. That's when I saw a very small tattoo of a crown at the small of her back. Marla was a Crown. Officer Dirk squeezed my hand.

"You going to be okay, Camp? You look dazed."

I wondered if my eyes were playing tricks on me. Pain pulsed in my head. My vision started to blur. When Marla went for another kiss, her shirt lifted ever so slightly again. I rolled over and looked under her shirt for just a second. This time, Officer Dirk saw.

"What are you doing looking up my girl's shirt?"

"She's a lesbian," Marla snipped, pulling down her shirt.

"What are you doing?"

"Time's up," Derrek opened the door and bolted in.

"So, are you coming to Mexico with me, Son, or do I have to drag you there?"

"We should go." Marla smiled.

"Oh, I bet that is exactly what the Crown want?" I said, laughing, feeling the tension lighten. "You are going to do exactly what they want and not even realize it."

"Stay out of this," Officer Dirk warned, lifting a brow. Suddenly, a gun was pointed at my face by Derrek.

"Pops, put the gun down," Jack shouted with deepening scowl. Officer Dirk stood. He was about to do whatever he had to, to protect me. He'd give his life to do it. I knew it. Officer Dirk wasn't afraid of dying like I was. He'd fight Jack's father and the entire gang. He was that kind of officer.

"Believe it or not, I am on Jack's side," I said. "You may not believe in him, but I see something in him. He'd make an excellent cop. He's got the skills, the brains, and the guts to do it. That is a rare combination. Jack would be the kind of officer I'd ride with. You are leading him from a good life. So is Marla. You can kill me if you want to, but I am going to die protecting one in my ward."

"Don't say that about my girl, Camp!" I just angered Jack.

"All I got to do is press the trigger, son."

"Marla is a traitor." I said. "She is trying to talk you into leaving the city just when you are in top of the world. You are unstoppable in that ring, and everyone knows it. You could get off in court if we speak on your behalf. You could have a good life."

"She loves me," Jack said. "No one has ever loved me like Marla. We've been together a whole year now, and we're going to get married someday."

"You tell her." Marla said. Officer Dirk was about to make his move. I knew his body language better than anyone. He just swayed on his right foot, which was readying his left hand for a hook to Derrek's jaw or chin, not sure which.

"You can kill me. But that's not going to change the fact Marla is a Crown," I shouted.

CHAPTER 19

I rolled over on the bed and rose the back of her shirt. In the center of her back, right above her buttocks, was a very small black crown. All Crown members get a tattoo to be initiated, and I knew what that meant. No Union gang member would ever get a crown tattoo because it would be seen as definite betrayal.

"That just means I'm a princess," Marla said. Her eyes filled with moisture as she brushed off the concern. Jack's eyes first showed horror, then betrayal, then complete and utter sadness. Derrick moved the gun from pointing at me to Marla.

"I'm not a Crown. That's crazy! I got this tattoo on my sixteenth birthday last year because my dad calls me princess. It has nothing to do with the Crown gang! Don't shoot me, Pops!" She cried out then, her lips pursed together.

"She's a Crown." Derrek's eyes welled up when he saw the devastation on his son's face. His rheumy, seeing eyes suddenly turned to fatigue and disappointment.

"How could you be a Crown and say you wanted to marry me?"

Jack started to cry.

"So that's why you wore a Band-Aid so much. You were hiding the tat!" Seeing his son so upset, his father lowered the gun and went to embrace him. Jack pushed him away, but his father sidled closer.

"I'll find out for sure."

"Marla's a Crown?" Jack repeated with a shaky voice.

"I'm not!" Marla had run for the door the second Jack's father held his son back from following her. She rushed towards the street. In a moment, the other Union gang members came into the room. One with a mole on his nose said, "You want us to get her?"

"You want us to stop her dead?" one asked with a quelling glance and a flip of his light brown hair.

Jack cried, "No! No more killings. Let her go. We let these officers go, and we fly out to Mexico. Okay? I'll go!"

"No, Jack," I said with a frantic pounding of my heart.

"You best think of yourself right now," Michael said with pensive eyes that studied Jack's every move. "We might actually let you all go. We could just leave them tied up, and then once we fly over the border, call in where they all are. No one has to die."

"Uncle is right," Jack said. "Our records are bad enough without officer blood on them. Since now, it's only been against the Crowns. We never had to kill no cops, Pops. I don't want to live with that on my conscience." Derrek started rubbing his son's back.

"So, we'll go to Mexico."

"You do that. You'll be a hunted man," I reminded with another glance of too-perceptive eyes.

"It's too late, now. We can't return to jail."

"Yes, Jack can," I said. "Officer Dirk and I will be sure to let the captain know what happened here. We can just go back to our jobs."

"We went AWOL, son. They would never let us do that now," Derrek said. "I'm so sorry about Marla. I should have known that she wasn't who she claimed she was."

"I never saw that tattoo on her back, Pops." Jack wiped his tears.

"Everything was a lie. All of it."

"Son, I will look into it," Derrek said. "It's no wonder why she wanted us to move so quickly to Mexico."

"You're falling into their trap. They want you gone so they can take over both sides of the city," Officer Dirk said. Jack continued to wipe his eyes when, suddenly, the door flung open. It was Captain McBride who had a gun in her hand. All the gang members raised their guns as well. Officer Dirk was mortified.

"What are you doing here?"

"When you didn't come back, I flipped on the tracker, and it led me here. Now I left a message at Juvie that if I didn't call in fifteen minutes to send in the blue shirts, so we get Jack back to the facility."

"My God, you've got guts, beautiful." Officer Dirk entered the living room. His expression softened the moment he saw her. Relief then lit his eyes. "But I think a decision has been made that they are going to Mexico, and all the cops get to go home for the night."

"Is that so?" Captain McBride saw me covered with blood on the bed. Her eyes widened. I sat up.

"I'm okay, Cap. It was the van rolling over that did this."

"What happened to your forehead?" she asked Officer Dirk.

"They did hit me with a bat," he replied.

"You, okay?" she asked him.

"Well, it hurts, but I'll live," he told her.

"So now you've come and stirred things up."

"Lower your weapons," Jack ordered his gang.

"This woman has a child at St. Jude's, and she's my friend." The gang members started to lower their weapons; the skinny one with blonde hair slowly dropped his gun; the one with the mole on his nose stuck his gun back into his pants; and then finally, the bald one carrying a large ax sheathed it back into his leather jacket. "He's gone soft," the bald one whispered. "I just had my heart ripped out of my body," Jack admitted.

"So, excuse me for wanting my friends to live. Union can go now. Leave before more cops come!"

"Now we've got a situation at juvie. We are surrounded by vultures, and at this moment, they are even scarier than all of you. So, let's go, Jack, get into my van and Camp with Dirk follow him."

"My son's not going back to jail!" Derrek said. Jack strolled over to his father and looked him in the eyes.

"I am, Pops. I don't want to do what the Crowns want. I hate Marla for what she did, but I'm not running. I don't want to live there. I want to go back. It's not too late. These people care about me."

"I care about you, son. I want you to live like a king."

"And not be able to live with myself. You're talking about killing people so we can rule in Mexico. I just want to finish school and maybe go to college."

"And what does a boxer need college for?" Derrek asked.

"I want to be a cop," Jack boldly announced. That was almost equal as saying he wanted to join another gang. The look on his father's face said it all. That was a horrible idea to him. His brother Michael patted Derrek on the back.

"Your son wants to be a cop," he said. "He wants to go to school and have a life of locking people like us up."

"Yes, Pops, so maybe it's me you should shoot instead of them," Jack said.

CHAPTER 20

erek's face reddened as he exhaled as he watched the Union gang members run out the door.

"Let's go," he said to the uncle.

"Let's catch the plane. I've heard enough." Michael and Derrek grabbed a few suitcases and headed out the door, ignoring Captain McBride's gun completely.

"Guess that was enough to have Pops leave me behind," Jack said. He grabbed a key off the buffet table and began unlocking the cuffs that tied the officers in the kitchen.

"He's setting them free?" Officer Dirk looked at me; then his eyes studied Derek as if he was uncertain Jack spoke the truth. When Jack got to the last officer, he swung around and began fighting with Jack, trying to restrain him. Jack quickly grabbed the officer's hands and whirled him around to face us in the living room.

"Tell him to back off. I'm going back to Juvie."

A blush washed up Captain McBride's neck; then she yelled, "Everyone stop!"

"You don't have any authority over us," the cop in Jack's arms said as he flinched. "We need to arrest him and go after his father."

Captain McBride said, "I am responsible for these two officers and that kid. I am in command at the moment. I suggest if you want to go after Derrek and Michael, then do it. You're wasting time with this kid. He's surrendered."

The moment she said that all of the officers who had been tied bolted out the door. Some started calling the escape in immediately, and before long, sirens sounded to announce the chase to stop Jack's relatives from leaving the state. I stood in front of Jack and flashed a weary grin.

"You're doing the right thing."

"It cost me my father," Jack said squaring his shoulders.

"Your uncle seemed okay with it," Officer Dirk said.

"That's because his sister is an attorney with the state department. She was going to help me with my trial, but I don't know if that's going to happen now," Jack said. "I may have done the right thing."

"You saved all of our lives," Officer Dirk patted him on the shoulder. "They probably would have killed us all."

"I have no doubts." Jack nodded and squinted. "But now doing the right thing may wind up with me in jail for stealing that car, killed by the Crowns, and losing my girl."

"She wasn't trustworthy anyways," Officer Dirk said. "And you, Cap, that was some mighty hero sh*t you just pulled off."

"I might have peed in my pants a little," she smiled.

"That was some SWAT-type stuff coming to save us," I said.

"Well, it was either that or let SWAT come in and try to handle the situation," Captain McBride said. "That would have only escalated the situation, and somebody could have gotten killed. Now we've got Jack; his father is going to Mexico. Good riddance, in my opinion. You really want to be a cop, Jack?"

"I thought about it after Camp suggested I'd make a good one."

"You'd be an official badass," Officer Dirk said. "But on the right side now."

"I already am a badass." Jack snickered with a gleaming platinum tooth. "I am tired of doing everything my pops wants. I realized I would never make him happy anyways."

"Let's get Camp and Dirk to the hospital, and then I'll bring you back to Juvie." Jack nodded.

"Sounds like a plan. I shouldn't be in trouble for going AWOL because I didn't know about any of this."

"I can verify that," Officer Dirk said.

"Okay, I have to make a report, but I'll record that you stood against your father and freed the other officers."

"Thank you," Jack said.

"I can't believe Marla is a Crown. I never would have guessed that in a million years. I met her outside my pops' boxing joint. No Crown ever comes within blocks of that place. She was standing talking to a girlfriend on the street. I'd never seen anyone so pretty in a pink dress and floppy hat. The hat was actually pretty stupid-looking, and I made some joke about if she got the hat at the Goodwill. She flicked me off. She actually had the balls to flick me off, and I smiled at her and lost it. I lost all my senses the moment she looked at me for the first time. Those blue eyes got to me. I stopped right then and asked her if she'd go to dinner with me at The Strawberry Mansion."

"That's where my husband Louigi works as a chef," I said.

"One of the fanciest places to eat on the Space Coast," Jack said.

"He must be very good. Marla and I went on our first date there, and I wanted to marry her right then. We talked and laughed for hours about everything and nothing all at the same time."

"I'm sorry," I said.

"This isn't really the time for your sad story, Jack," Captain McBride said.

"Awe, Cap, he's heartbroken," Officer Dirk understood.

"Well, he has plenty of time for his heart to mend at JDC. He needs to get back to the facility as soon as possible, or I'll never be able to explain how long it took us to get him back. I don't want this to get back to headquarters because I could lose my job. I got a little boy who needs me to bring home a paycheck."

"We hear you," Officer Dirk added. Then Captain McBride lifted her hand, pointing to the door. We all trailed after Jack and got into the Juvie transport van that Captain McBride had driven to get there. We drove several miles until we got to the hospital where Officer Dirk and I got out in front of the emergency room. The moment we walked in the hospital, nurses surrounded us and put us on stretchers. Officer Dirk asked for us to be placed in the same room, and they obliged us so we could stay together.

"I don't think he will give any trouble too, Camp," Officer Dirk said to me.

"I know. He's a good kid," I said. "Surprisingly."

Officer Dirk turned on the television, and there were scenes of vultures attacking people in front of a school.

"The world seems to be ending," Officer Dirk said.

Before long, I got a blood transfusion which made me feel so much stronger, almost as good his new. Officer Dirk did not have a concussion, just a nasty bump, and we were told to take it easy for a few days by the hospital doctor. Both of us knew that wasn't going to happen. Officer Dirk grabbed a taxi out front, and we headed back to Juvie without even a break to speak to our loved ones. A part of me knew if I told Louigi what all happened here today, he would insist I come home immediately. I wasn't about to let that happen with all these vultures flying around town. Every few minutes we would peer out into the skies, worried that the vultures were nearby, but it was growing dark, and if they were in the skies, it was hard to tell.

"I am going to sleep in the breakroom," I told Officer Dirk.

"You take the sofa, and I'll take the brown chair," he said.

"Deal. We can switch halfway through the night," I said.

"You, feeling better?" he asked me.

"Like brand new, minus a few stitches," I said.

"Now all we've got to worry about is bloodthirsty vultures," Officer Dirk said.

"No problem. We'll have the taxi driver pull into the garage, and it's not like they can get into Juvie," I said. Officer Dirk gave me a look that he was indeed worried that the birds could somehow get into the facility.

"One battle at a time," I said.

"It sure seems like it's the end of the world," Officer Dirk whispered.

"The end of the world."

CHAPTER 21

ouigi begged Captain McBride, "You better let me speak to Laura, or I am going to come there myself to check on her."

"Laura is fine. She's doing her rounds. I'll have her call you as soon as she's done, Louigi." The friendliness on her face vanished as she clutched the phone.

"You said that an hour ago," he said. His throat got so tight he spoke like a whisper. "Let me speak to my wife now! Something is wrong. I can feel it."

"All right, then," Captain McBride said gathering her wits. Her high-range voice quivered. "I'll put you on hold and stop what I am doing to go get her."

"I'll wait," Louigi said, and then music started on the phone. Captain McBride sat back in her chair and watched the blinking light on the phone by the word "Hold."

"You better hurry your ass back from ER," she said to herself, "or he'll be here before you get back." She looked at the clock across from her desk. Fifteen minutes had passed before the phone light disappeared. She called the front desk.

"If Louigi calls me again, stall him on the phone. Camp will be back any minute."

"He's called ten times," the woman reminded. Her expression had gone sober and calculated.

"Camp is on her way. Once she gets back with Dirk, we'll have her call him, so he stops worrying," Captain McBride shot a stern glance.

"He said he was coming if we didn't put Laura on the phone," the front desk informed.

"He said the same to me," Captain McBride said, and the back of her neck prickled. "Let's hope he doesn't come. If he does, she'll be here by then and will never know how much I lied."

Across town, Louigi jumped into a beat-up pick-up truck. Doofus was in the window barking. A frown appeared as Doofus stared back at him through the window disappointedly.

"Sorry, buddy, you can't come on this ride. Don't worry, I'll bring Momma home though." Louigi started the engine and sped off. He flew down the roads. The skies were too dark to see if there were any vultures in the sky, but he did see a few perched in some low trees and on electric lines. Seeing them only fueled his fire to get to the juvenile jail as soon as possible. Something in his gut told him his wife was in danger. That's when he pulled out a kitchen knife from out behind his belt. He didn't own a gun, but this knife could kill any big bird with one quick slash. It was the sharpest knife he had.

"I'm coming, Honey," Louigi said. The interstate was empty. Not a car or truck in sight, and that's when he saw the highway sign overhead flashing. **Stay off the roads. Mandatory Curfew. All residents to stay indoors until further notice. Blockades at Camp Road.**"

"So you think a few blockades are going to stop me?" Louigi placed the knife on his dash. "I'm coming, Laura."

Wouldn't she be pissed at me if she knew I was coming! Louigi thought to himself; that's when he remembered his wife's physical test to become an officer. It was at the sheriff's training facility. Not far from the gun range was an obstacle course that every person who wanted to graduate had to pass in a certain time or limit to earn their certificate. Back then, he knew not only could she run the course in time, he knew she would do it in half the time. He had sat in the bleachers watching all the men struggle up the rope to ring a bell at the top. Then they had to crawl on their bellies underneath barbwire before jumping a fence. This was not an easy course, and every weekend for the past six months, Laura had come here to train it as quickly as possible. That day, she was only one of three women to attempt it. She was given one more minute than the men to pass, and instead of Laura liking that, she was pissed.

"I don't need an extra minute!" he recalled her saying. "I'm going to do this faster than any guy as it is."

***

When the gun fired off and about half a dozen men and three ladies started the course, Louigi wasn't worried. Laura ran faster than everyone. She jumped onto the hump and crawled up it, ringing the bell with no worries. Underneath the barbwire, she crawled so low to the ground that she wasn't in any danger of being scratched. No, Laura was in front of the pack at every turn and corner. By the time it came to climb the fence, Laura was breathing heavy, but she nearly flew over that fence. At one point, Laura glanced back to see that no one was even close to her. Apparently, all those months of training and jogging at the gym had paid off. Laura rang the final bell, two minutes before any other man. She had beaten even the sheriff's record for the obstacle course. Everyone applauded when Laura finished that course. It was apparent to all that she would make a superior officer. Louigi was so proud of her, he rushed across the field and gave her a big kiss.

"I am so proud of you!" he said. It was then that Laura nearly cried. She didn't cry then, but she did at graduation, and then again when she was hired by Captain McBride.

***

"McBride is such a liar," Louigi said to himself. "She's in trouble. She never goes this long without checking in."

98

His truck moved to get off the exit from the highway. It was then a giant black vulture hit the windshield of the truck with a loud *THUD*! Blood flew all over the windshield, and it was all Louigi could do to keep his truck on the road. He slammed on the brakes. "Holy crap!" Louigi took a deep breath. Then he turned the wheel to pull back in the center of the highway exit. "Got one."

CHAPTER 22

From his back pocket, Louigi's cell phone rang just as he turned right toward the prisons.

"Hello," he answered. "Laura?"

"No, it's her mother," her voice sounded panicked. "Laura's not answering her phone. I've been calling all night."

"I know," Louigi announced. His eyes widened. "She called me to tell me the facility was on lockdown and after the boxing match she would have to go back to the facility for the night. I've been calling there, but they won't put her on the phone."

"Something's not right. This isn't like Laura not to call me for so long. What do you know about the vulture attack?"

"Laura told me that none of the kids were hurt, and the person who was killed was an animal control officer. She claimed that everyone was safe inside. I am headed to JDC right now, and a vulture just ran into my windshield."

"Are you all right?"

Louigi wiped off his dash. Something in the air made him shudder as a headache began to throb his temples. "Yes, but there is glass everywhere inside my truck. I'm not sure I care much about this truck damage, though. We were planning on getting me another truck to use for gardening.

"You took the red one," she asked.

"Yes, so not a big concern at the moment."

"Do you have Doofus?"

"No, he's at home. If something should happen to me and you can't get a hold at Laura, please check on Doofus."

"Don't worry," Lucinda said, clutching the phone. "I will go in the morning to make sure he's fed. Will you make sure to call me once you see her and tell her to call me?"

"Yes," he said. He paused, then said softly, "Try not to worry."

"I've been worried since she put on the badge," her mother admitted as her pulse galloped. "Oh, that was a day, wasn't it?"

"It was." Suddenly his mouth shot into a triumphant grin. "You were so proud of her."

"Her father had to ruin everything at graduation," she said.

Louigi shook his head and then gained a bit of courage to say, "Actually, Laura was glad he showed up. I know it upset you greatly, but it mattered to her. She did reach out and invite him and her grandparents."

"Her grandfather was a cop in Brookhaven for over thirty years. She grew up listening to his stories. This is his fault!"

"You need to let your hatred of them go," Louigi said as one hand clenched. "I've got to go. It looks like there are some bushes in the road. I'll need to get out." With that, he hung up the phone. *That was quite the day.* He recalled when Laura was in line to get her diploma. Instead of robes, she had on a blue corrections officer uniform, and when she got in front of the line, they gave her a badge. Laura was beaming ear to ear. He hadn't seen her that happy since their wedding. He was seated next to her mother. As she got her badge, he quickly took a picture. She was so beautiful. He was so proud of her because she had gone to the academy and worked so hard to be at the top of her class. That wasn't easy for a woman. He knew her grandfather had been a police officer, and he arrived in full uniform for her graduation. After all the students went through the line, Louigi and her mother hurried over to her. Her mother didn't see her father approaching or the man in full uniform standing beside him. When she did, Laura's mother couldn't hide her disgust.

"I'm here for our daughter," he said with a quick look, and then he studied the room full of people.

"I invited them," Laura told her with her smile fading. The grandfather gave her a hug with tears in his eyes.

"You make the family proud."

"Thank you," Laura said, touching his arm. "I remember when you used to play cops and robbers with your cousin," he said, glancing her way with a question in her eyes. "You always arrested him and then stuck him in the clubhouse behind the house. We should have known then you would become a corrections officer."

"Awe, Grandpa." Laura swooned. "I am so glad you came. We're all going to dinner to celebrate. Can you and Dad come to Roadhouse? My treat."

"Absolutely not!" Lucinda grimaced. "Mom, this is my graduation."

"Can't you let it go for once," the father said. "My cheating on you happened ten years ago. I'm remarried to Carol now. I've moved on."

"Good thing you can," Lucinda said. "Who never sent child support? You should be in jail. You are nothing but a deadbeat father who has the nerve to show up now after all these years. You didn't even come to Laura and Louigi's wedding."

"Actually, I didn't come because I knew you didn't want me there, but I did meet Louigi and Laura the night before and gave them a gift."

Lucinda's eyes widened.

"Yes, Mom, Dad sent us on that cruise to the Bahamas," she told her. "I didn't tell you because I knew you wouldn't want me to accept it, but we have forgiven Dad, and I want him and my grandparents to be a part of my life now."

"She takes after me." the grandfather turned to Laura's mom.

"Please let all of this anger go."

"That's easy for you to say. You didn't have to raise a child on one income and barely scrape by while he stuck his dick into anything that moves."

"Mom!" Laura stopped her. "Everyone can hear you."

"Let them hear. You've come all this way not because of him but because of your hard work, Laura. You are the one that studied hard, did the obstacle course over and over, and took all those combat classes. You are your own woman!"

"That's true" Louigi interrupted the fight. "Laura did this even without much help from anyone. She did this because being an officer is what she wanted. She is a strong, independent woman, and she got that way because of you." Suddenly, Lucinda's eyes filled with tears.

"I just want to be here now to see this," Laura's father said.

"Please, just one dinner," the grandfather said.

"We love Laura, too."

What a dinner that turned out to be! Ended up in screaming matches, but we were all together then. I'd give anything for that again now! Laura's got to be okay!

CHAPTER 23

Louigi got out of the truck cautiously. He looked up at the skies, and the nearby trees seemed to be playing tricks on him. Shadows were dancing everywhere. He hurried to a large bush that had tumbled into the center of the road. He picked up the bush and dragged it toward the side of the road. When he turned around, he couldn't believe it. On the hood of his truck were about half a dozen black vultures. One was on his open door. They were staring at him, with beady eyes following him as he left the bush. His knife was still on the dash of his truck. He had to make a decision then. He could try to swat them away, start the truck, and try to get to the facility, which wasn't far away now. That was one idea, but the look in their eyes certainly made him think twice about that. He took another step closer. One opened his wings as if to warn him to stop.

"Nice birdie," Louigi said, and admitting to himself he was afraid which felt like weakness. Another step, and another vulture opened its wings and squawked, and then it was game over. All the birds flapped their wings and flew at him. Louigi ducked and started to run in the opposite direction. He knew exactly where he was. There was a park down the road. A small fishing cabin was there, and it was open to the public. He'd run as fast as he could to the cabin and lock the door. Angry at himself for not grabbing the knife or his phone, he continued to run as fast as he could. Louigi knew he was not the athlete his wife was. No, he preferred eating food and cooking it than any of these restrictive diets his wife was on. He regretted that now that his life was on the line. He heard the birds flapping their wings above him. They were very close. He looked back and saw them flying only feet behind. Their claws were outstretched as if ready to bounce on him at any moment. He ran through two trees and heard one crash into it. Perhaps that was a strategy to try to outrun or outmaneuver them. Out of the corner of his eye, he saw a cabin. There was a man with a fishing pole sitting on the dock.

"Hurry!" Louigi screamed. "Get inside!"

The man jumped up and opened the door of the cabin just as Louigi rushed in. He slammed the door on three that smashed into the door. "They were after you!" the man said.

"They're diseased," Louigi told him; his eyes held amusement mixed with fear.

"Name's Frank." The older gentleman held out his hand and looked past his shoulder at the birds in the air. He placed his fishing pole on the side of the room.

"I'm Louigi Camp," he introduced himself, hearing more birds hit the door. He held his smile even though he was hiding the chill running down his spine.

"Looks like you are lucky to be alive," Frank said.

"What are you doing here? Isn't the park closed?"

"Well, yes," Frank said with a content expression. "I come here every night after my wife finishes dinner. I just come here to have some peace and quiet. I'd heard about the vultures being dangerous, but I thought it was some crazy talk."

"Not so crazy," Louigi said as his brows drew together.

"Where did they all come from?" Frank gasped.

"Didn't you know about the curfew?"

"Yes," Frank said sounding disappointed. "I went around the police blockade the back way. I didn't think vultures were actually attacking people. I thought the whole thing was about a prison break or something the reporters just made up, some vulture nonsense. I've been on this earth nearly seventy years, and vultures don't attack people."

"They do now," Louigi said with a frown.

"You know, I did find it odd that they were circling around that JDC facility," Frank said.

"My wife, Laura, works there," Louigi caught his breath and sat down on a sofa made from wood and cushions. "That's why I'm in this mess. I was trying to get to the JDC, and there was a bush in the middle of the road. Then the vultures attacked. I remembered that this fishing cabin was here and ran as fast as I could."

"I haven't seen anybody but you," Frank said with softening eyes, "so I don't know if your wife is there or not."

Suddenly, a vulture slammed into the window. It cracked all the way across the center. One more hit like that and the birds would be inside the house. Then Louigi noticed the fireplace. He ran to make sure the chimney shoot was closed. By the time he got to the latch, one of the vultures was in the cabin. Frank grabbed his fishing pole and began swatting the bird as hard as he could.

"Take that!" Louigi patted him on the back the second the bird stopped moving.

"Great job, I think it's dead."

"But my pole didn't make it," Frank showed him that the tip was broken.

"How about when we get out of here, I buy you a new pole?"

"Oh, you don't have to do that," Frank exhaled.

"It's the least I can do," Louigi said. Before he could fully see the pole's damage, the front window smashed in as a vulture flew through it. Dozens came in flapping their wings and with their claws outstretched. Louigi did what he could, striking out at them. Frank screamed as they clawed at his face and belly. He hit as many as he could with the fishing pole. He took a few steps out onto the porch as Louigi dropped to the ground and went under the sofa.

"Hide, Frank!" Louigi cried out. Then Frank let out a horrible cry and fell back onto a chair on the front porch. Louigi saw vulture after vulture coming down onto Frank through the window. He was far enough under the sofa and yanked down the cushions to protect himself from them coming under. Slowly, he closed his eyes; he didn't want to watch the vultures tear Frank into little pieces.

CHAPTER 24

Doofus was half asleep on his doggie bed next to the front room recliner. He was happy to get some quality time on his extra sofa pillow his human mommy Laura had brought to him not long ago. The pillow was the softest thing in the entire house. Next to that was his water bowl with his name carved into the holder. He heard a creak coming from the kitchen. One of his ears popped up, because it sounded like his doggie door opening. He heard another noise and his head jumped up. *Yes, that was my doggie door opening!* Doofus jumped to his feet and headed to see what had entered his territory. He was not happy about anyone invading his turf! As he entered the kitchen, he put on the brakes and slid into the kitchen cabinets. He couldn't believe his eyes! A giant black vulture was climbing through his door. This had never happened before. He remembered how one had chased him all the way inside when he was out with his parents. The door still had a crack from the last one. Doofus barked. He didn't approach, but he would try to scare it away. The bird opened its wings and hissed loudly. That freaked Doofus into a barking frenzy. Even his growling didn't stop the bird from hopping toward him. It was the bird's beady black eyes that suddenly made Doofus turn and run. The safest place in the house was under Mommy and Daddy's bed. The bird was too big to fit under there, he hoped. *Mommy and Daddy, come home!*

Doofus ran as fast as his little legs would carry him under the bed, where he whimpered and crawled into the back corner. It didn't take the vulture long to get inside the bedroom and stick his head underneath the bed. He tried to peck at Doofus, but his neck was just a few inches too short. Doofus barked loudly and growled. He had nowhere else to run but out the other side and into the bathroom, so he ran there as fast as he could. Then he remembered that with his nose he could shut the door. When the door slammed, he was so proud of himself. He could stay here until his parents came home. They couldn't be gone long, and he sure felt safe. Suddenly, he heard that horrible hissing sound again from above. Slowly, Doofus looked up, and that's when he saw the vulture sitting on top of the wall ridge. Oh no! He had forgotten that the doorway didn't go all the way to the roof. The vulture knocked down a plant which landed about a foot from his left paw. Now the door was shut, and he was in the bathroom with a vulture above him. The vulture started tapping his claws against the ledge. They made a horrible scrapping sound as he raised his wings.

"Get out of here!" screamed Lucinda as she hit the bird with a large broom. The blow knocked it to the ground. Then the door to the bathroom opened, and Lucinda pounded the bird over and over until it was a bloody mess, no longer moving. Lucinda bent over and picked Doofus up. He was so happy to see his grandma that he covered her in licks all over her face. He knew she didn't like them on the lips, but he didn't care; he was so happy to see her. He knew Grandma had just saved his life.

"How did that nasty thing get in here?" Grandma led him around the house until she saw the doggie door cracked about an inch. Lucinda quickly put Doofus back on the floor and latched the doggie door. She pushed on it to make sure that it wouldn't budge open again. Inside her purse, she had a doggie pee pad, and she put it on the floor.

"Gotta stay inside for a while, Doofus. Like when you were a puppy!"

Lucinda grabbed a pair of gloves from under the kitchen sink and a garbage bag. It didn't take her long to pick up the dead bird and stuff it into the bag. She whistled while she worked, carrying the bag into the garage where she stuffed it into the trash. Out there, she grabbed the bucket and mop. She went back to the bathroom and filled the bucket with soap and water. Before long, Lucinda was mopping up the blood from the floor. Doofus tried to get closer, but Lucinda gave him a look, and he knew to wait outside the door. It took her quite some time to clean up the mess from the floor and then the spatters on the walls. It wasn't an easy clean up, but Lucinda continued to whistle and sing a song Doofus didn't understand. He may have almost lost his life, but Grandma was there, and everything seemed better again. Lucinda dumped the water back into the bathtub. It was full of blood.

"There's no saving this mop," Lucinda told Doofus; then she went back into the garage, left the bucket, and stuffed the mop into the trash. "I hope the garbage truck comes soon, or that's really going to smell."

Lucinda reentered the house and went and sat on the sofa. Quickly, she turned on the news, which was full of reports of vulture attacks and warnings to stay indoors. The curfew would continue until further notice. "Looks like we're in for a long night," Lucinda said as she patted the spot on her belly, the squishy part of Grandma Doofus loved the most. He jumped onto Grandma's lap and curled up into a ball as she watched television. It didn't take long before she started to snore. Doofus was very happy she was here, and then he heard a familiar sound which made him rush toward the door. *Ding dong* went the doorbell.

CHAPTER 25

Doofus was a good guard dog because he knew when to bark. He ran to the door and got louder as Lucinda approached to see who was at that door.

"Who is it?" Lucinda tried to see through the pinhole opening. A shudder made its way down the back of her spine.

"It's Derrek," came a voice Lucinda hated.

"Go away, asshole!" Lucinda roared at her ex-husband. The color drained from her face.

"I'm looking for Laura. I keep calling her phone, and she's not answering. I just want to make sure she's okay with all these vulture attacks. Is Laura there?" A truculent expression crossed his face.

"That asshole, son of a bitch!" Lucinda said as she unlocked the door. She whipped it open and heaved a sigh.

"Get in here; we just had one try to get Doofus."

Derrek's eyes widened, and then he patted Doofus who smelled his hand. He must have recognized the scent because he started wagging his tail and stopped barking.

"You okay, boy?" Derrek asked him in a shaking voice.

"He's fine. Don't you see?" Lucinda scoffed. Something shifted in her eyes. Lucinda shut the door.

Derrek began calling out, "Laura! Laura!"

"She's not here," Lucinda said. Her lips twisted in anger. "The JDC is under lockdown until further notice, and Louigi is with her. I think. At least that's what he last said to me. He was on his way there when he asked me to come feed Doofus in the morning if he couldn't get back."

"So why are you here now?" Derrek asked. Then he lapsed back into silence.

"I thought I'd spend the night," Lucinda said. "Doofus isn't used to being alone for very long, and I worried about him going outside to pee. Good thing I did. One of those blackbirds came right in the doggie door. Doofus would have been a goner had I not come when I did!"

"Where's the bird?" Derrek looked around.

"It's in the trash," she said as a hand fluttered to her mouth. "I killed it with a broom, which is what I will do to you if you don't leave immediately!"

"Oh, stop." Derrek suddenly gave her a brilliant smile as his brow furrowed. "You actually killed one with a broom?"

Lucinda melted a little when she saw that smile. She suddenly realized that what she had done was a bit brave. "I did, asshole."

"Will you please stop calling me that?" He laughed, then gave a brilliant grin. "Laura sure takes after her mom. So fearless you are. You came right in here and saved the day."

"Could you imagine Laura and Louigi without this dog?"

Derrek shook his head and pushed out of his mind a fearful image of Doofus dead. "Nope."

"I just did what was necessary," she said, nodding. Suddenly, Derrek leaned over and gave Lucinda a kiss on the cheek. It surprised her at first, and then her eyes tightened.

"What the hell are you doing?"

"Thanking you," he said.

"Thank me with a beer, not one of those kisses that used to always get me in trouble."

"Still a feisty one." Derrek padded over to the fridge and pulled out a Corona. He grabbed the beer opener from a drawer and popped it open for her.

"Your favorite, Lucinda." Lucinda took it from him.

"Can I have one?" He reopened the fridge.

"Aren't you leaving?" Lucinda said.

"Don't you think it would be nice for us to sit down and talk. We haven't talked more than two minutes since our divorce, and for the most part, that's been mostly you calling me names."

"I don't like your company." Lucinda returned to the recliner. Doofus jumped back onto her lap, and she began to pat his head. "But I guess a few minutes wouldn't hurt. I am very worried about Laura and Louigi. I haven't heard from either of them, and neither are answering their phones, which isn't like them."

"I know," Derrek rushed over and sat on the sofa next to Lucinda's recliner. "It's not like Laura not to call me on break."

"She calls you on break?" Lucinda was surprised.

"And sometimes my father, too," Derrek said.

"Well, she always did like that man. She grew up listening to all his cop stories. It's no wonder why she wanted to become an officer."

"Her goal is to help those kids," Derrek reminded. "Did you know she really wants to study forensics next? Solving murders, rapes, and all that horrible stuff. Who wants to do that?"

"Our daughter," Lucinda smiled. "She turned out good, Derrek. Even with all she's been through, and YOU put her through. She turned out good."

"She's a good person, Lucinda," he said, proudly.

"A good wife. She's loyal to Louigi. I've never seen a couple more in love," Lucinda said.

"Sometimes they remind me of us. The way we used to be, Lucinda, before I cheated on you. The good years, those ten."

"They weren't all that good," Lucinda grimaced. "You snored so loud some nights; I could barely sleep especially when you were drunk."

"You were hardly a drinker then," Derrek said.

"I got my high out of life then," Lucinda said. "I was happy for the most part."

"You know, Lucinda, Laura is worried about all your drinking and that you have no interest in dating anyone either."

"Who'd want me?" Lucinda scoffed.

"How can you say that?" Derrek took the drink out of Lucinda's hand. Doofus cocked his head as Derrek leaned in. "You are still the most beautiful woman I have ever known, Lucinda. You have a soul like no other. It's golden."

"Asshole," Lucinda whispered just as he kissed her cheek.

"Please find it in your heart to forgive me. Those ten years were the only years in my whole life I was ever loyal to a woman. That's because you were the only woman tough enough to keep me in line."

"What about Carol or the other one?" Lucinda asked.

"Cheated on both my other wives," Derrek admitted. "See, it wasn't you that was the problem, Lucinda. I have a wandering eye. You were the only one that I ever loved, too. I have never felt about a woman the same way since. I made a mess of my life, Lucinda. None of what happened was your fault. It was mine. I am so sorry. I am sorry for cheating and messing up our marriage. I shouldn't have, and I shouldn't have broken Laura's heart when she was just a little girl. I'm so sorry."

Lucinda's eyes filled with tears. "You really mean that?"

Derrek nodded yes. "With all my heart, Lucinda."

"You're still an asshole." Lucinda smiled.

Derrek kissed her cheek again, "I know, but right now we need each other. I don't know about you, but I am scared to death for our kids. I am praying Louigi and Laura are okay. Thank you for saving our little friend here, too." He patted Doofus on the head. Lucinda wiped her eyes.

"I love this dog, too."

"Forgive me?" Derrek asked.

"No," Lucinda admitted. "But I could use a friend right now, I suppose." Derrek stood and went to sit down beside Lucinda.

"Good, then we'll wait this thing out together. One of them is bound to call one of us soon." Then they both fell silent and watched the news of another vulture attack on TV.

CHAPTER 26

aster Control was full of officers. It seems all the JDC employees for the state of Florida were gathered to find out the latest report on what had occurred. At the front near the surveillance screens stood the wildlife and game officer next to Captain McBride.

"My name is Donald, and I am the supervising general manager at the Wildlife Commission Office. I want you all to be aware that the bird that was captured is now on its way to our veterinary laboratory in St. John's to be studied. We will find out what is the cause of this strange behavior." I wasn't sure who was responsible for this bird mess, but I was tired already and wanted to rest in the breakroom. Being in this meeting was the last thing I desired.

"Most of the birds have returned to the dead pine trees outside the facility," the officer continued. He must have seen the desperation in Captain McBride's face because he placed a hand on her shoulder.

"Only a few other reports of people being attacked in parking lots have been reported. So, in some respects, we are lucky to have most of these birds in one area. It could be a lot worse."

"That is why none of you are allowed outside other than in the garage to get into the vans," Captain McBride interrupted. Her voice vibrated with authority.

"So far they haven't attempted to enter the garage."

"Possibly because of the strong lights," Donald said. He frowned and warned through gritted teeth. "But don't go into the garage unless you absolutely have to."

"Don't need to tell me twice," Officer Dirk mumbled.

"We also have another situation. One of the animal control officers told his wife about our little problem here. That normally wouldn't have been a concern, but she emailed her boss, and now our entire mess is public. It wasn't just the *Sun* reporting on our dire situation with all these attacking birds."

"Who is her boss?" I asked.

"The local paper," Captain McBride announced shaking her head.

"Not only was the last attack headline news in the *Sun*, it's all over Space Coast News and the internet by now. The main focus of their stories aren't even the bird attacks but that Jack the Mack, the national boxing champion, is facing his biggest opponent yet with these vultures. We keep getting calls from newspapers all over the world wanting to interview Jack."

"Do they know yet of his escape from prison?" I asked as the dread slithered up my spine.

"No, not yet," Captain McBride said. She closed her eyes briefly.

"They don't know about the kidnapping and the attempted escape by Jack either. We don't need any more out there. Believe me!"

"Have any more reporters arrived?" Officer Dirk asked with a sigh.

"We have a feeling they'll be just like a hurricane. They will not heed the warnings to stay away, and a few might eventually show up. We need to be prepared for that," Captain McBride said.

"So, we need to be concerned about the safety of the press as well?" I wondered tucking my hair behind my ear.

"This is quite a story."

"The police department has quarantined about five miles in every direction. They've stationed a few police cars to enforce that. So, let's hope the press won't become an issue." Captain McBride caught my hand movement.

"We do have to worry about your husband, Camp." She was looking right at me.

"My husband?"

"Louigi has been calling ever since the news hit the internet. He's, how can I put this mildly, freaking out, and insisting on coming to the facility to talk to you."

"Oh no," I breathed with dry mouth, suddenly needing to regain my balance

"I took one call and tried to explain that you are fine. He told me that he's coming down here to see for himself since I wouldn't put you on the phone. I even warned him of the roadblocks, and he said…and I quote… 'Nobody is going to stop me from checking on my wife.'"

"I'll call him," I said, nodding. "My phone is in my locker."

"I wish I didn't have to tell you that I believe it is too late for that," Captain McBride said.

"I already got a call from the police while you were being released from the ER. Your husband drove through the roadblock in a red pickup truck and headed down the dirt path past Sarnino Extension."

"That's a mile dirt road. He'll be here any minute," I said with pounding heart.

"It was nearly a half hour ago that I got that call," Captain McBride said. "The truck hasn't been seen since. I'm now very concerned that something happened to your husband."

My hands clutched my hips as chills went down my spine. Every inch of me ached at the very thought of anything bad happening to Louigi. He was the love of my life, but even I knew that nothing would stop him from checking on me. I couldn't even imagine a day without him, let alone lose him to some crazy peckers! He owns no weapons. That beat up ol' truck was something that he used on the weekends instead of taking out the sports car. It was so loud at times; we should have been able to hear it. No, the truck was stopped somewhere, and it was too dark to see the birds in the sky.

"What I am telling you is that now we need to plan out a rescue for your husband," Captain McBride said. "We need to have two officers go in one of the court vans down the dirt path and see if they can find him. It could be as simple as the truck might have run out of gas. He could have been blocked by a fallen tree after that storm we had a few weeks back. I don't know. Just get your ass in that van and bring him here and don't take a heck of a long time to do it."

"I'll go with you, Camp," Officer Dirk volunteered. Captain McBride stopped him.

"You will do no such thing, Dirk. You are to stay here. Our first situation is to keep these birds away from our kids! I need as many officers in this facility as possible. The kids are scared, and when they are scared, they don't behave. You are one of our best."

"Thank you for wanting to help me," I told Dirk. "But it's fine. I got this."

"Captain, I insist. It probably take us just a few minutes to find Louigi. She's my partner, and if something is wrong, I know how she reacts. We know each other like the back of our hands. She might need that kind of backup—we are a team." I realized then how actually worried he was to think we may need to be in combat and know each other's moves. Captain McBride's eyes suddenly turned to fear. She liked Officer Dirk more than she ever let any one of us know.

"Let me do this," Officer Dirk pressed. "She's my partner."

"All right, Officer Dirk and Camp will take a van into the woods and try to find Louigi before any of the birds find him or them." Captain McBride said, gulping. "This better be the only spouse missing, too. I want all of you to take a five-minute break and call your homes, explain to your loved ones that the stories on the news are exaggerated and that everyone here is fine. We don't want a panic on our hands of all the parents of the kids in the cells, right?"

The officers nodded in agreement.

"Leave immediately." Captain McBride looked at me. "But be back as soon as possible. We need to be prepared for anything, reporters or parents in a panic."

Officer Dirk said to me, "I'm sure he's fine."

"He better be," I muttered.

CHAPTER 27

As I drove one of the transport vans, Officer Dirk was making sure his window was closed on the passenger's side. He kept looking up at the sky with a worried expression written across his face. Quickly, we barreled down the dirt road behind the facility to where they had last seen my husband, Louigi. Officer Dirk was silent. All I could hear was the air conditioning in the van. My stomach was in knots. The thought of never seeing my husband again made me sick inside. I remembered when I was in criminology class at our local community college, I was so nervous then when I was about to take my final. Two years of classes riding down to one major exam. If I failed, I wouldn't get my criminology degree and be able to take the job at the juvenile facility. We wouldn't have been able to put that down payment on the house, and the loan wouldn't have gone through. Instead of going alone, Louigi offered to go to the college and sit in the pavilion in the center of the college buildings. His being there meant the world to me. It helped me overcome all my fears. Seated inside the pavilion, I could see him from any of the windows of my classroom. When I sat down at the desk, I glanced over and saw him smiling up at me. Just seeing him there made me more comfortable. He sat down at one of the round picnic tables and fed a squirrel. A few of them darted from the pine trees down to meet him, hoping to be thrown some peanuts. I got to a question I wasn't sure was the answer. My eyes moved back to the pavilion, and Louigi was there watching a large white egret who was walking on top of the schefflera bushes. He'd tilted his head and grabbed a lizard among the yellow and green leaves.

"Five minutes," the proctor alerted. Quickly, I jotted down my answer to the last question. I handed in my test and hurried downstairs, across the grass to the large pavilion. I cleared my throat and swallowed a lump. I sat down next to him as the egret continued to eat a bug and draw closer. What a stunning white bird with long orange beak and tall black legs. In the Florida seventy-degree winter breeze, the bird turned its crooked neck while the long, white feathers rustled in the breeze. Louigi reached down and held my hand as a train a few blocks away blew its horn. The crane didn't seem bothered by us or the train. Its only interest was the little brown lizards jumping from leaf to leaf.

"So how did you do?" he asked me.

"I think I got an A," I said with my lips turning into a skeptical twist.

"Onto the next class in Crime Scene Investigation then." He smiled.

"We can't afford me to continue my education right now," I reminded, digging at the truth. "I want to get married and buy that house."

"You could get another student loan," he said, slapping his hand against his forehead.

"What about you going to culinary school and getting your certificate next?" I smiled, glimpsing yearning in his eyes. "It's your turn. I want to take the JDC job for now. I want to help the kids get out of a life crime."

"You want to do CSI work?"

"I know. Eventually, that's my goal. I'll work as a JDC officer for a while until you're a chef, then I'll go back after you get a job at a fine dining restaurant or one of the beach resorts." He kissed my cheek and went silent for a moment.

"How'd I get so lucky?"

The van hit a bump in the dirt road, bringing me back to present time. Louigi wasn't holding my hand. Beside me was Officer Dirk, clearing his throat, his eyes peering out through the glass up into the sky. The birds he was searching for were nothing like that beautiful white egret crane. In front of us, about a hundred yards up the dirt road, I could see Louigi's pick-up truck among the trees. The driver's door was open. The front windshield was cracked and half laying on the ground.

"They got to him." Officer Dirk gasped. His words slurred.

"Do you see your husband?" Suddenly, my hand landed down onto the horn. Honk! Honk! Honk! The noise was loud enough to be heard half a mile away. If Louigi was anywhere around, he should be able to hear the honking of the van. Honk! Honk! Honk! I hit the horn of the van, again and again. My heart was pounding as my eyes searched through the trees and around the bushes. The van slowly approached the truck, but he was nowhere to be seen. Flying above were several vultures high in the sky. One, hearing my horn, landed on a nearby oak tree.

"The noise is attracting them," Officer Dirk warned, then forced his attention back to me. "Stop it!"

"I want Louigi to know I'm here."

"We should drive around. He's probably hiding," Officer Dirk said suppressing a sigh. Suddenly, a fat gray cat dashed out from underneath a bush. The vulture in a nearby oak flew down and snatched the cat by his tail. The cat hissed. It whirled around at the vulture and tried to claw its beak. The vulture flew up, breaking the cat's tail, making it crooked. The cat cried out in pain and ran underneath our van, hiding from the cruel big bird.

"Wow, Jerry finally got Tom!" Officer Dirk said.

"This isn't funny," I scoffed with a frown.

"My husband is still missing."

"At least we know he's not dead, or his body would be here," Officer Dirk said curtly. I started the engine and moved slowly forward. The cat ran underneath the van until we got close enough to a bush. Then, it darted out, just missing our back tire, to hide inside the bush. The vulture swooped down at it, again, but the gray cat with the crooked tail went between the branches.

"Lucky cat," Officer Dirk said.

"Now he's got a broken tail."

"Better a broken tail than a dead cat," he reminded.

"I'm praying for a whole husband." I sighed, then pressed my lips together. Officer Dirk patted my shoulder.

"We'll find him. Don't worry. He's somewhere close by. Isn't there a park just around the bend?"

"Yes!" I gasped. Louigi and I had been there a few times. It was a small park with a few benches, and there was a cabin with an outhouse. Louigi might have gone there to hide.

CHAPTER 28

Officer Dirk and I headed toward the cabin. Even from this distance I could see that the small wooden cabin had been attacked. The winders were broken. In the doorway lay a fisherman, his hand holding a pole with a dead vulture stabbed through the belly. The smell was hideous. My hand flew to my nose in an attempt to stop myself from gagging. In the doorway, I called. My eyes searched for a proximity.

"Louigi!"

"Maybe I should go back and keep honking the horn," Officer Dirk said.

"Let's check this place out." I slowly walked in the open doorway and studied the space. It had four wooden bunk beds, a small wood-burning stove in the corner of the room. From the broken windowpane, I could see the creek. It wasn't a large creek, but it ran all the way to St. John's River and was known locally for having lots of rainbow trout.

"Don't think he caught more than the vulture," Officer Dirk commented. He cleared his throat, and a hint of fear flashed across his face.

"I used to fish that river as a child," I said. Remembering caused a warm shiver down my spine. "My dad and I would take a canoe and go down the creek for hours. We caught mostly trout, but that was before my parents' divorce."

"Not me. I used to come here as a teenager with my older brother." Officer Dirk smiled. "Just catfish, but one time my brother saw a water moccasin."

"Those are a plenty around here."

"Let's get out of here," Officer Dirk said. "Your husband isn't here. We're better off driving around and honking. Maybe he will hear it and come out of the brush." Wham! Something grabbed my leg. My gun came out, and I pointed it toward what had snatched my leg. A hand coming out from the lower bunk closest to the door.

"Come out with your hands up!"

"It's me." Louigi rolled out from underneath. "Shhhh, they keep coming back to make sure no one else is here."

"The birds?" Officer Dirk questioned with a frown.

"Yeah, every fifteen minutes one would fly to the window and then fly off."

"Are you okay?" I studied the frightened expression on his face and swallowed hard.

"I'm fine," he said as faint as a whisper. "Better than Frank the fisherman. It looks like they got him before he could get inside."

"What happened to your pick-up truck?" Officer Dirk questioned searching his gaze.

"They attacked it. I've never seen anything like that since Hitchcock's movie *The Birds*." He gasped. "I ran as fast as I could here. I thought I'd be safe, but they got the fisherman by breaking the window."

"Maybe the odor of the dead fisherman is masking your scent," Officer Dirk concluded. Louigi wrapped his arms around me and kissed me.

"What's going on at the center?"

"A wildlife officer was killed," I informed. A pang struck me, but I pushed it away. "Another one did capture a specimen, and the vulture is being tested for disease."

"It could be a virus," Louigi said while shooting me a glance.

"I suppose."

"We're not sure of anything other than the vultures' behavior is dangerous enough to kill several people now," Officer Dirk said. I smiled at my husband, glad to see him and thrilled he wasn't hurt.

"We should go back to the facility and report the fisherman's body to the police."

"I love you," Louigi said.

"Now and forever," I replied. The vultures were circling the skies but over the facility about a quarter of a mile away. We hurried back to the van. Just as we got inside, one vulture broke from the flock and smashed into the cabin's window.

"That's the one," Louigi said. "I was sure he'd find me eventually." Louigi sat behind me as I started the engine and drove the van back down the bumpy dirt road back to the facility. My eyes were stuck on the skies, which were nearly black with hundreds of giant vultures circling above. Why were these birds focused on our facility? So, they tasted human blood? Do they want more? What was attracting them, and why were they now attacking the living?

"Pinch me," Officer Dirk murmured.

"I think we're caught in a nightmare."

CHAPTER 29

The three of us headed towards the van. When we crossed the path of Frank the fisherman, the view of the body was hard to take. What surprised me the most was that, with all these vultures in the skies, there was still some flesh on his bones. In his hand lay still the fishing pole. Around his feet, a few dead birds. They may have gotten him, but he took a few out as well. Officer Dirk leaned down and started touching the body.

"That's evidence you're messing with," I reminded him as a headache pulsed at my temples.

"Even though I think you'd make a great crime scene investigator someday, now is not the time, Camp."

"You looking for something?" Louigi asked shooting a quick glance.

"A phone," Officer Dirk replied with weakening voice. "I want to make sure Cap knows we found you and that we're still alive."

"It might be in his coat pocket," Louigi said with furrowed brow.

"Right above the lung that is half hanging out of the ribs."

"You had to point that out," Officer Dirk said as his hands went into the pocket of the coat.

"Well, if I had a coat like that, that's where I'd keep it."

"Hurry up." I saw the vulture in the window staring at us.

"It's looking right at us like we're next." I pointed to the huge bird. Then the vulture let out a horrible cry. Birds began dropping from the sky and surrounding the van.

"Got it! Let's go!" Officer Dirk pulled out a phone from his pocket. All three of us ran for the van. Louigi ran for the back, slid the van door, and jumped into a seat. I jumped in the driver's side, and Officer Dirk quickly got into the passenger's side. I quickly locked the doors and started the engine. Officer Dirk immediately called Captain McBride's private number. His admiration seemed to morph into something more serious.

"Cap, it's Dirk. We found Camp's husband, and we are headed back."

"Any injuries?" she asked.

"No, I am happy to report the three of us are fine, but the vultures did kill a fisherman at the park. We don't know his identity."

"I'll call it in," Captain McBride said.

"The cops had to leave the blockades because the vultures kept trying to break in their windows," Captain McBride announced. "So we need you two back here. It's only a matter of time before reporters and parents start coming."

"Oh, Mom!" I looked at Louigi and tucked my hair behind an ear.

"I spoke to Lucinda about going to the house in the morning and feeding Doofus." I gave Officer Dirk a look and outstretched my hand as the van took off down the dirt path. Surprisingly, the birds seem to be following the van. They'd land a few trees in front and then move as we did.

"Hitchcock, anyone?" Officer Dirk said goodbye to the Captain and handed me the phone. I then passed it to my husband. My eyes lit with amusement.

"Can't call. I'm driving." Louigi laughed.

"Yes, let's not forget about the phone laws while driving." He took the phone from me and dialed his mother-in-law's private cell phone.

"Hello," Lucinda answered.

"It's Louigi. I am with Laura, and we are headed to the facility which is still on lockdown until further notice. She is right next to me, and I'm putting you on speaker phone."

"Is she all right?" asked Derrek in the background.

"Put yours on speaker phone, too."

"Wait a minute," Louigi said with widened eyes.

"Are your parents together?"

"Oh, that's not good," I said firmly.

"Yes," Lucinda answered as she put her phone on speaker so both could be heard.

"We are at your house. It's a good thing I came over because the doggie door was open, and a vulture tried to eat Doofus." Louigi and Laura's faces curled in horror.

"Is he all right?" Louigi asked.

"Yes," Lucinda said.

"She killed the vulture with a broom," Derrek informed them sounding proud.

"So, Doofus is good?" Louigi asked repeatedly. Doofus barked when he heard his father's voice.

"Now you've got him all excited," Lucinda added.

"I put down some pee pads, too, so Doofus wouldn't have to go outside."

"We'll stay here till you get back," Derrek said.

"So don't worry about Doofus. We'll take good care of him."

"What about you two, my parents, being together, in the same house, without killing each other or my dog?"

"We're fine," Derrek said.

"Don't worry about us. We are so happy you two are okay! We've done nothing but worry. When Laura didn't pick up her cell phone, I thought the worst and came here to get answers from Louigi."

"My phone is in my locker," I said. "We had the fight last night one of our inmates was in. The facility is still being attacked, so until we find out what's going on with these birds, we're not being able to leave yet."

"Is Louigi going to stay there with you?" Derrek asked.

"Yes, Pops, I am. I am never leaving again until I know she's safe from these birds."

"Okay," Lucinda said.

"Can you keep calling us then? So we won't worry so much?"

"Yes, Mom." I smiled as the color started to return to my face.

"We'll check in. Now you two behave until we can come home. Take care of Doofus."

"No problem," Lucinda said

"We've got it. Don't worry about a thing. Just take care of what you need to do at work, and we'll hold down the fort." Officer Dirk moved his hand to hang up the phone, but I interrupted with "Love you both" before he could.

CHAPTER 30

I drove the van into the holding garage and pressed the button for the giant metal door to close. The door rolled open, and Captain McBride's large frame stood in the doorway.

"Good, you're back!" she said.

"I'm going to stay here with my wife," Louigi told her.

"You can stay in the employees' lounge. There is a sofa in there, television, and I'll bring you food trays." Captain McBride walked over to the van. Her expression changed.

"It has blood on the side."

"Not sure if we hit one," I said. My lips trembled, so I pressed them quickly together. "But there is a dead fisherman in the cabin down the road. His family needs to be notified."

"It's already been reported," Captain McBride said. "We got another problem as well. The boxer's uncle just showed up here, and he is refusing to go without talking to his nephew, Jack."

"You need our help?" Officer Dirk questioned.

"Camp and Dirk, head down to Jack's cell. I still need to fill out the paperwork about your finding a dead man at the park cabin."

"Louigi, can you go to employees' lounge?" I asked. "I got to get back to work."

"Our casa is su casa." Captain McBride smiled and rubbed her chin. "I'll show Louigi where it is."

"Thank you." Louigi smiled, but his voice was resigned.

"Camp can see you on break," Captain McBride assured him. Officer Dirk put in the door's code, and we hurried down the corridor to where the prisoners lined up to enter the cafeteria. The kids were scared. They were trembling and wide-eyed. Jack was in the center of the line. Next to the fighter was Jack's Uncle Michael sitting on the floor. He appeared just as he did in the farmhouse wearing the same clothes. Next to the man was Officer Gilman, who didn't look the least bit pleased. His hands were on his belt as if ready to pounce on Michael if he made any moves.

"Wasn't he going with Jack's father to Mexico?" Officer Dirk questioned as he shifted uncomfortably.

"Captain McBride already gave Michael five minutes to check and make sure Jack was fine with all the television news reports about the vultures. The next problem is now Michael is refusing to leave without talking to him again."

"I won't leave my nephew," Uncle Michael grumbled to the two officers as they approached. The words nearly froze the blood in my veins. As I went around to the side, I could see that Michael had tears streaming down his face. His features were similar to that of the Jack's, with the same long face and solid jawline.

"He's safe inside these big cement walls."

I hesitated, then asked, "Is Jack's father gone?"

"He's on his way to Mexico," Michael said with narrowed eyes. "I couldn't leave Jack here in America without protection from the Crowns or the vultures." Jack put his hand of his uncle's shoulder and said in a choked voice,

"Don't you see this is embarrassing me?" He pointed to the Crown gang members in line to the cafeteria. "I am fine."

"Please, Jack, listen to me. You need to hear my words and understand what I am trying to say to you."

"Listen to Jack," Officer Dirk said with a scowl.

"Whatever your personal problems are, they'll have to wait. We've got a serious situation here, and the facility is on lockdown. If you want to stay here, you'll have to get permission to stay in the lounge. Otherwise, the police will escort you back home."

"It's the end of the world," one of the Union kids said. "We're all going to die. Just let 'em talk to Jack."

"Quiet," I ordered.

"No talking until you get your food and sit down."

"I heard the birds can get in through the windows above the cafeteria," another of the juveniles said.

Officer Dirk explained, "All the glass is bulletproof. The windows are all locked. Our walls are thick. Nothing, unless we let it, gets in here."

"Jack," his uncle grimaced. "I spent half my life behind bars. I don't even deserve a nephew like you, and I am so proud that you want to become a cop someday."

"Leave me be," Jack murmured. "I don't want anything to do with you. Where have you been all my life that now you want to help me? Just go be with my pops."

"I know." The man wept.

"I deserve that. I came to make you see, to beg you, don't live your life like us. Learn from our mistakes. If I could change what I did, I would. Jail isn't the life you deserve. You're smart. You're talented. You have skills that I never had. You can make something of yourself more than a life inside a steel cage."

"I didn't even want to take that car," Jack answered.

"I didn't rob that lady either," one of the kid's interrupted.

"They're all innocent." Officer Dirk placed a hand on the uncle's shoulder.

"You need to get up and come with us to talk to Captain McBride. Perhaps she'll let you stay in the employees' lounge if you are worried about Jack's safety."

"I promised his father that I wouldn't let Jack out of my sight."

"Didn't he leave his son the second he heard he wanted to be a cop?" Officer Camp asked.

"His father wouldn't be able to live with the worry that comes with being the father of an officer. It would put a mark on him. No one would trust either one of us." The uncle's eyes reached mine. He nodded, and then his attention turned back to his Jack. "I am begging you. Do the right thing. Don't be like us. Don't ruin everything that's going for you. Stay in school. Get a scholarship and make something of your life. I love you. I stayed away for a reason. I didn't want you to wind up selling drugs like us for the Union. I kept my life away from you for a reason."

"I ain't nothin' like you or Pops." Jack the Mack grimaced. "I ain't nothin' like you. But I don't want either of you to die because I go back to school to become a cop either."

Louigi was escorted by Captain McBride into the employees' lounge. There were a few recliners and a sofa. The television was turned onto the news. A few snack machines and a microwave and refrigerator sat in the corner.

"It ain't much, but it's home for now," Captain McBride welcomed Louigi with gentleness in her voice. On the sofa was a little boy about seven years old. He was wearing a blue jumpsuit with a train on it, and his head was bald.

"This is my son, Douglas," Captain McBride added with a quick glance. "I had the hospital bring him here so I can keep a good eye on him. He finished his set of chemo for now, and I couldn't leave him alone." Louigi went over to where the young child was playing. In his hands, was a Yoda stuffed animal.

"Hi, Douglas," Louigi greeted, his eyebrows rising to almost his hairline. "You like Yoda?"

"Chewy is my favorite," he said softly, then looked away. Louigi got down onto the floor and crossed his legs. He hoped he would accept his ambivalence.

"I like Chewy, too. I've seen *Star Wars* over fifty times." Douglas's eyes widened, and he wrinkled his nose.

"That's a lot of times. Do you like Marvel, too? I love the Avengers!"

"I prefer Loki." Louigi smiled, glancing at the boy's shirt. "Nice train."

"Thank you." Douglas grinned. "You have blood on your shirt."

Louigi hadn't even noticed. His voice held its edge.

"I'm sorry. It's not mine. Don't worry. I am not hurt."

Captain McBride interrupted, changing the subject.

"Will you be okay in here with my friend Louigi?"

Douglas nodded yes.

"How long will you be working? I want to go home."

"I'm sorry, Sugar," Captain McBride said as she wiped her face.

"We're on lockdown, but you will be just fine here."

"Can't I go home?" Douglas said, and then his stomach rumbled. Officer Dirk walked in and saw Douglas. He immediately reached down and gave him a huge hug.

"Hello, Douglas."

"Dirk," he screamed in glee. "Can you play *Star Wars* with me?"

"Can, I not," Officer Dirk imitated the voice of Yoda. "The cafeteria, I to go."

"Now what?" Captain McBride asked biting her lip.

"Michael, Jack's uncle, doesn't want to leave Jack. Apparently, he promised his father to look after him."

"We're not a hotel," Captain McBride said with a shrug.

"We've got room," Louigi interrupted. Captain McBride grimaced and closed her eyes for a moment.

"I suppose we do for now, but it won't be the Waldorf Astoria for any of you. I do understand people wanting to be with their loved ones."

"This is kind of like a hurricane," Louigi said with a nod.

"Except with birds instead of wind and floods."

"I suppose we can make room."

"Jack and his uncle did make sure we weren't killed by the Union."

Louigi grimaced, "I think he can be trusted, and Jack doesn't want to go AWOL. He wants his freedom."

Captain McBride patted her son on the head. Her voice turned soft and barely recognizable. "I don't like this. But these are dire times. Normally, I'd keep my son away from criminals, but I don't want him at home with just my mother either. We don't really have a choice other than to call the cops and have Michael removed."

"That will just make things worse," Officer Dirk said with a quick glance. "We'll keep an eye on him, too. He's still talking to Jack. Apparently, the reason the father didn't want Jack to become a cop was that it could put a price on his head."

"They'd never trust any of them again," Captain McBride concluded. "If he joins, it marks them with the Union."

"We need to keep Jack on the right side of the law." Officer Dirk gave her a wink. "I think his uncle wants that, too, even though there might be serious consequences." Captain McBride suddenly reached out and hugged Officer Dirk and her son in her arms. At first, Officer Dirk was surprised by affection in front of others.

"You okay?" Officer Dirk asked her.

"I am just very thankful that we are all alive," Captain McBride said. "If we all get out of this, I'll buy you a beer, Dirk."

"That would be my pleasure." Officer Dirk nodded.

"I enjoy spending time with you and your son."

"Thank you." Captain McBride hugged him longer this time. The hug was lasting so long that it made Louigi uncomfortable. Then Douglas left Officer Dirk's side and went back to sit next to Louigi. He smiled up at him.

"My momma likes Dirk," he whispered, "But, shhh, don't tell, because they work together." Louigi glanced up at the two of them still in each other's arms.

"I won't say a word to nobody."

CHAPTER 31

"That's right," the uncle said to Jack. His Adam's apple bobbed in his neck. "You're nothing like us. You've got a future with boxing. You could get a scholarship to a good school and become a police officer. You're smart, and you are making better choices." Jack the Mack rolled his eyes.

"At least you got a dad and an uncle that care about you," the young man said next to him. His face was full of trepidation. "Mine killed himself when I was six. Shot himself in the head because he lost his job and my mom started cheatin' on him."

"I'd rather kill myself than let one of those birds get a hold of me. They are straight from hell," another youth said, wiping the back of his hand across his mouth.

"I'd rather die."

"Don't say that," I interrupted as Officer Dirk returned to stand by my side.

"I ain't got much to live for anyway," he said as his gaze skittered.

"I'm going to the big house."

"Are you Crown or Union?" I asked him. The young man showed me the back of the elbow which had a tattoo of a crown. His eyes narrowed.

"I'd never be Union."

"After you get out of here, I heard what they are gonna do to you," Jack the Mack warned with warning plastered in his eyes.

"I heard you slept with the wrong lady, too." Officer Dirk gave me a look. I've seen that rise of the brow before. Officers have to take threats like this very seriously. It's more than just making sure these kids are safe in here. We try to help them, rehabilitate them, show them that they have more options.

"You willing to make a statement to the police?" I asked Jack the Mack, my smile faltering. The young Crown member laughed. Hatred and rage mingled into a visual kaleidoscope which left his mouth sagging.

"He won't help me. He's Union."

"If you do, it will be mentioned in court that you helped stop a potential murder or assault of an inmate," I said taking a deep breath, then focusing on his face. Jack the Mack looked down.

"You help him," the uncle ordered. He blinked and then with a frown said, "It will help you get out of here."

"Like I said, Uncle"—Jack the Mack grunted with exertion—"I don't help anyone in the Crown."

The Crown member leaned against the wall as if he already knew that the boxer wouldn't help. However, I wondered if there might be another reason.

"If you help him, would it put you in danger with the rival gang?" I asked, feeling frozen in place.

"What do you think?" he whispered. His uncle harrumphed and stood, nearly punching the wall.

"Son, you've got to rise above hatred and these gangs. That's what I told your father, too. You've got to turn your back on both and become the man I never was. You hear me?"

"Why should I do anything for you at all? You were never around until Pops became head of the Union. Remember? Drugs meant more to you than me!"

"I wanted you and your mother to have a better life. The money was rolling in. I thought that was how to do it. I was wrong. I paid for my crimes with ten years in jail, and nothing will ever bring that back. The years I missed watching you grow wasn't worth any amount of money."

For a moment, Jack nodded in agreement. Then he straightened, staring his uncle in the eye. His smile seemed genuine.

"All right, I'll make a statement to the police. I'll even tell him what I heard at the club. I don't think that it will do much good."

"You'd do that for me?" the Crown member gasped.

"Why not? You're dead anyway."

"Don't be so sure," I said. "All right. We'll set that up, and we'll be sure to tell the judge of your willingness to help stop a possible murder. That might help the judge see you in a new light."

"No need." Jack sniffed. "I'll be out of here in no time."

"And go back to school," his uncle took a step back. "I'll be there to see you walk and get that diploma."

"You were right about a mark being put on our backs if I become a cop," Jack nodded. "How can I do it knowing it would get us killed?"

"How about becoming a sports physical therapist? Didn't you mention that you wanted to know more about that to help you when you become a boxing trainer? Your mother wrote me when I was in and told me that. They make great money. Regardless of your boxing, it would help you with learning how to treat injuries."

"Useful information," Officer Dirk said.

"Who cares about that?" one of the kids said. "We're all dead! We're all going to die! Those vultures will get us all! We're going to hell."

Officer Dirk moved over to him. "Come with me. No class after lunch for you today. I'm calling in the mental health counselor."

"I want to die!" he said. "They ain't gonna get me."

Michael moved over to the young man who threatened to commit suicide. "Don't say that. I saw three men hang themselves in prison. You've got lots to live for, even in a place like this. You've got a life outside this place yet to live."

The young man raised the sleeve on his shirt and showed him his Crown tattoo. "I don't want those vultures to get me!"

"Wow, Uncle, you're all kind of caring today. Giving advice and all."

"All right," I said. "He's going to the mental health counselor. You, sir, are leaving to go into the employees' lounge with a police escort. These kids need to eat before they have class."

"Hey, thanks, man," the Crown member said to Jack.

"I mean that."

"I don't help Crown gang members," Jack snipped.

"I'm just doing it because it's the right thing to do."

"That's a boy." Michael started walking towards the front of the facility.

"I may be your nephew," Jack said, "but you're still a pain in the ass with all this advice."

Taking a step toward the cafeteria door, I smiled. "You should learn from his mistakes and become a better man."

"That won't be hard to do," Jack said.

"At least your uncle came here today," I reminded.

"He must care somewhat."

"For now, until he's back on drugs." Jack went into the cafeteria. I've heard plenty of stories like this. The young men and women who come on the inside usually have parents that were in and out of jail or basically don't care much about their kids at all. Most of them are products of being ignored or watching their parents do crime. Every once and awhile you get a bad seed who just wants forever to do crime, but for the most part, a lot of them are doing what they can just to survive.

Michael was escorted into the employees' lounge where he surveyed the large room. Louigi was still playing with Douglas on the floor and watching the news. Michael saw the sofa and immediately went to lie down.

"Hello," Louigi greeted.

"Do you know what time it is?" Michael asked him.

"It's one," Louigi answered. "You must be Jack's uncle, Michael?"

"Yes." Michael reached out to shake his hand. "And you are?"

"I am Louigi. I am the husband of Officer Laura Camp."

"You're the one that disappeared, and they brought back. So, is it true?" Michael questioned.

"About the vultures killing another man in the park?" Louigi closed his eyes for a moment. "It was quite awful."

"You saw it?" Michael asked.

"Yes, it happened very fast. They tore him apart with their claws in a matter of a few seconds."

"That must have been horrible," Michael consoled. "Did you know him?"

"No, he was just going fishing and minding his own business. One minute alive, the next dying as he fought them off."

"He died an honorable man, fighting until the end." Louigi was quickly reminded that the man he was talking to was a criminal.

"Yeah, I suppose that is one way to look at it. I ran under the sofa and pulled down the cushion so they couldn't get me."

"You did what you had to survive," Michael said.

"It happened very quickly," Louigi said. Michael's warm smile disarmed Louigi. His stony expression softened.

"I'm sorry," Michael said. "You have to let go of things like that. There was nothing that you could have done. These things are out of our hands. Something is making these birds go crazy, and we'll all be lucky to get out of this alive." Louigi shrugged.

"We're safe in the facility more than if we were out there. These walls are three-foot thick cement, and the windows are bulletproof, so they can fly into them all they want to. We're better in here than out there. We got food, drinks, and a place to sleep in safety inside these walls."

Michael said, "Safety is an illusion, my friend. Never forget that."

Louigi was handed the Yoda stuffed animal from Douglas.

"Yoda likes you."

"I'm not much of a Jedi," Michael said.

"You could be," Douglas said. "Jedi, you will be."

"I hate that Yoda guy." Michael crinkled his nose. "Not all of us want to be Jedis or listen to his incorrect English. You shouldn't talk like him, boy. He speaks all jangly and wrong. You shouldn't admire something that's short, green, and with such ugly big ears."

"He is not ugly," Douglas snipped, jerking his head around. Louigi was surprised by his short fuse.

"It's okay, Douglas. I like Yoda."

"Yoda may be short, but he's one of the most powerful things in this universe. He'll protect us from those birds and so will my mommy."

"Who's Douglas' parents?" Michael asked him. "Is he yours and Laura's?"

"No, Douglas is Captain McBride's." There was something very engaging in his eyes, and then Louigi's voice softened.

"What's he got?" Michael questioned him.

"I got cancer," Douglas told him. All the pain of the diagnosis washed over his young face like a wave of terrible memories. "But I am going to be fine. That's what they told me at St. Jude's. I just got my cancer treatment last week, and it is going to be my last because my tumor is almost gone."

"You are a brave little one," Michael suddenly said with enthusiasm.

"Yes, and so is Yoda."

"So is Yoda," Michael agreed. "I am sorry I called him short and big eared." His voice sounded slightly weary as he rubbed his temples.

"There's nothing wrong with being short or big eared." Douglas thrust out his chin, and his lips turned into a straight line. "We can't all look alike, especially in this universe."

"You're right about that," Michael said. "I guess I don't like him because I am with Darth Vader."

"Darth Vader is dead." Douglas scowled. "The emperor killed him with his lightning fingers. Luke couldn't save him."

"Wow, he knows his *Star Wars*," Michael said. "Those movies came out long before you were ever born."

"My mommy watches them all the time. She likes Lando. She thinks he's hot."

Louigi laughed. "I thought she likes Officer Dirk."

"Him, too." Douglas chuckled. "Now you be Yoda, and I'll be Luke. You can train me to become a Jedi."

"You already are," Michael sighed, then bit his lip.

"You beat cancer." Douglas looked over her shoulder at him. He flushed and nodded without hesitation.

"I did."

"That's a scarier thing than anything Yoda ever battled. Cancer is the ultimate Darth Vader in my book." Captain McBride entered the employees' lounge.

"I need you to sign some papers, Michael, that if anything happens to you in here, you won't sue the state." Michael took the paper out of her hand and walked over to the table. He pulled out a chair, sat down, and signed the paper with a few quick strokes of a pen.

"You guys think of everything."

"Just procedure for anyone staying in the employees' lounge. And, by the way, neither of you is to leave this room except for the bathroom across the hall. Got it?"

"Got it," Louigi said being handed the same paper. Louigi stood and went to the table. He sat next to Michael and signed the bottom as well. Then he grabbed Michael's paper and his own and returned them to Captain McBride.

"We got no worries," Michael said, pointing at Douglas.

"We got a Jedi with us."

CHAPTER 32

Four men loaded themselves into a truck. One was tall, with tattoos all over his arms, including a big crown on his forearm. On his head was a baseball cap which was plain white. The second one looked like he could be in prep school with tight jeans and a polo shirt that didn't hide his enormous arms or the tattoo of a crown on the back of his hand. He pulled out a gun from behind his belt and stuck it on the dash.

"That's all you're bringing?" said a man with dark brown deadlocks. In his hand, he had a larger gun. A tinkling soft laugh came.

"Awe, snap, Jake." His stare intensified.

"You're a Crown now, Garrett. You've got to know how to roll." Jake's scowl tightened his mouth. The truth began to sink in.

"Got any weed on you, Jake?" his gaze questioned the preppy Crown member to the one sitting in front of him. The last of the four opened the back-passenger door and sat down. He was short, bald, and wore a blue jean jacket. On his neck was a Crown tattoo.

"Jake ain't got no dope, but I do." He opened his jacket and handed it to the preppy Crown member. The sudden smile did not cover the shadow in his eyes.

"Thanks, I want to get high before we get to Juvie." His gaze searched Jake's face. "They won't know what hit them," Garrett said.

"Look what I got." He pulled out an AK-47 machine rifle with a warning expression.

"What do you need a military rifle for?" asked the preppy one.

"Shut up, Sal," Garrett said to the preppy one with a lump growing in his throat. "This thing will get us through that door. It will take down anything, even bulletproof glass." Sal nodded as the truth sank in.

"We got to do what we got to do to save our friends."

"None of them can go to court," Garrett reminded, sounding authoritative. "The blue are cracking down on the Crowns now that Jack is their golden boy."

"Jack will get off because he raised money for that children's hospital," Sal said.

"The cops are taking down the Crowns when they should know the Union are the frauds trying to kill us off."

"We got Jack with Marla. He had no idea she was one of us," Jake said, grinning to lighten the mood.

"All she needed to do was talk him into leaving the country."

"It should have been Canada," Garrett said, his voice heightened by his agitation. "I bet they could have talked him into going to Canada instead of Mexico."

"At least his father left," Jake said, flipping his dreadlocks over his shoulder, tightening his bulging muscles.

"We know that for sure?" Sal wondered, rubbing his bald head with worry shadowing his eyes.

"Yeah, he left for Mexico and left Jack unprotected from the Crowns."

"So, we take Jack out and we got the run of the whole city?" Sal questioned.

"That will make things easier when we get the next shipments."

"We can take over the girls, too," Garrett said.

"They are working too hard for way too little profit. We will take over the streets entirely, and the Union will eventually fall apart or join us."

"You think Jack needs to be killed?" Sal asked Garrett. He pushed back his jacket.

"I can slice 'em and dice 'em once we get to Juvie."

"So, what's the plan?' Jake turned to Garrett. "We just show up and start hitting the door with the AK?"

"The door can't withstand that many bullets," Jake said.

"Then we go to the left, and that's where the cells are. We get them to release all the Crowns, and then we will get Jack before we go. That's how we take over the city. The Union won't expect it. Jack won't be able to fight back if we get him inside the cell."

"How do you know so much about Juvie?" Garrett asked Jake as he continued to rub his bald head.

"You shining that thing?" Jake laughed.

"You should let your hair grow out like I did."

"You don't even wash that," Sal snipped.

"No, thanks! It smells like shit, too."

"Hey, men pay thousands to have their hair look like this," Jake said. "The reason I know so much about the layout for Juvie is because I was once there about ten years ago. I was just a boy then."

"Will they recognize you?" Sal wondered.

"No, I was just a boy when they put me in the hole. That's solitary, and it's a living hell not to be able to see anybody or hear anybody." Jake shook his head. "I am happy to put holes in that place and get our brothers out."

"Sorry, I brought it up," Sal said, rubbing his head one last time. "I do this when I'm nervous."

"Relax." Garrett took a hit of the dope. "You've got us. We've got your back."

"And you sure that they don't have any guns?" Sal asked Jake.

"Yeah, nothing but tasers and batons," Jake reassured. "They won't be able to do a thing because of our guns. It won't even take fifteen minutes for us to bust down that front door and get our brothers the hell out of that place. They won't make their trials either. We are the judge and the jury. Crowns don't pay for their crimes. We get paid." Sal pulled out his huge knife.

"That's right. Me and my girl are ready for anything."

"Your knife is a girl?" Garrett asked Sal.

"This is Sally, and she likes to cut anyone who gets in my way."

"Nice," Garrett nodded. "We might need Sally once we get inside."

"Let's hope not." Jake moved his dreadlocks away from his eyes.

"The goal here is to get in and out before any cops can come to the JDC. The quicker the better. We'll just go in there and take our brothers."

"What about those vultures all over the news?" Sal wondered.

"You're worried about birds?" Garrett laughed.

"Yeah, what are they going to do, peck us to stop us from getting our crew?" Jake laughed heartedly. Sal chuckled and put Sally into his denim jacket.

"Yeah, I guess you guys are right. We need to worry about the officers trying to stop us from getting our brothers, not a bunch of vultures."

CHAPTER 33

Suddenly, the lights went out. Gunshots hit the front doors, bringing it down piece by piece. Code Red. The facility was under attack, and the alarm blared. The surge of adrenaline quickened my pulse. The emergency lights flickered on, and Officer Dirk and I screamed at all the inmates in the facility, "Cells now!" His voice booked no argument. "Now!"

Captain McBride called over the intercom. Her voice demanded, "All officers secure your position. We are under attack by four assailants outside the front entrance. The police have been alerted and are on their way."

I'd seen things like this on television, but it seemed surreal now that it was happening. Besides holding off winged creatures, we would have to fight off armed assailants. Every moment suddenly seemed like I was moving in slow motion. All of the inmates ran out of the cafeteria, down the hallway, and into their cells. Once we saw them secured, I motioned for the doors to lock, and all at once they locked in sync. All of the inmates were secure, but Officer Dirk and I headed back toward the front of the facility while hearing the gunshots. For a moment I glanced over at Jack in his cell. He had no fear in his eyes. His uncle ran out of the employees' lounge. Louigi was with him.

"What's going on?"

"Get back to the lounge and lock the door," I ordered impatiently.

"I stay with my nephew," he said, then paused and wiped his brow. "Open his cell, and I will wait in there." I went to put the key in the lock and a hand shot out from the food tray opening, grabbing at my wrists.

"I'm here if you need me," Jack said, confidently.

"Are these assailants here for you?" I asked him. My smile dimmed. He gave me a rude look back and released my wrists, then shrugged. *Could this day get any worse?*

Captain McBride had locked three officers in the bulletproof control center just outside the front doors. Officer Dirk and I moved to the side hallway across from the cells so we could see to the north entrance but be just out of sight. From the corner, we watched the front north entrance door fall to the ground in three big pieces. Inside the facility walked four young men in their teens. They were all different races. It was hard to tell that they were a gang except all four sported giant crown tattoos on their upper shoulders or neck. Yup, the Crowns were here probably to break out their own and kill Jack. The four began shooting at the officers in the glass control center, but this time, the glass held. Captain McBride said over the intercom.

"The police have been called. Leave now, and you might have a chance to escape."

The muscular one in the center with light brown dreadlocks and blue eyes roared, "Open the cell of Mark Knight and Jack the Mack." Rage lit his dark eyes. He barreled ahead, then bit his lip.

Officer Dirk got closer to me and whispered, "We should go outside and take them from the back." He handed me a taser. Slowly, I grasped the taser gun in my hands. I took it. I'd been here for years and never held a gun; now I've held two in the last twenty-four hours and witnessed two dead men. In horror, I realized that may just be the beginning. Then I remembered Louigi was in the employees' lounge, alone. The four gangsters were nearly down the hall from where my husband was.

"We don't have time," I said, moving closer to the corner of the hall. It was inches away from where I could be spotted.

"Free Crowns now!" Jake snarled as his dreadlocks fell over his shoulders. He glowered and glanced at Captain McBride. I checked the cell where they were being held with smiles on their faces as if they knew that this would happen.

"You're not getting out of here."

"You better let us out," he said with a fake smile.

"We don't release prisoners here."

"You're gonna regret that," one said showing me his Crown tattoo; then he leaned down and screamed through the food tray slit,

"Here, all the Crowns are down here."

All four of the gang members turned and headed closer, that is, until they saw me and Dirk at the corner. Three of them raised their guns while the fourth moved back to keep an eye on the control center.

"The Union have to do something, or they're dead," Jack told his Uncle.

"Let the Union out of their cages," Michael said to Officer Camp.

"You're crazy to face four! That's Sal, Jake, Johnny, and Garrett. They're all killers."

I shook my head no. "That gangster ain't worth your life." Michael gasped.

"Justice is worth my life," Officer Dirk said, steeling his resolve.

"If I didn't believe that, I wouldn't wear a badge." A part of me thought it would be easy to let the Union out of their cells and let the gangs fight it out. Or would they? It was then I realized.

"What's to say that they don't kill us all after we release Union?" Suddenly, the one with dreadlocks put his gun on the floor and came walking around the corner, three feet away from us, staring us, eye to eye.

"I'll shoot you," I said, holding out my taser. A twinkle lit my eyes, proving I would pull the trigger. "If you make one more move toward that cell."

"We come in peace," Jake laughed then muttered, "And we'll leave with everyone in pieces."

Then I saw Louigi opening the employees' lounge door. His eyes bulged the second he saw the four gunmen pointing their guns at Officer Dirk and me. He stared like a deer in the headlights. The four of them didn't see him open the door, but they did see little Douglas go between his legs and walk right in front of the four gunmen. Douglas walked right in front of them and stood in front of Officer Laura Camp and Officer Dirk.

"Go back inside the lounge," I said to the boy sharply.

"I'm your only chance," Douglas said.

"What do you want?"

"We want all of the Crown gang members released, and we're taking Jack the Mack with us," announced the Crown member with dreadlocks.

"That's not going to happen," I said matter-of-factly. Suddenly, the doors to the control center opened and in ran Captain McBride; risking her life, she picked up Douglas right in front of all the gunmen.

"Is he yours?" Sal asked, the light glistening off his bald head. Captain McBride's eyes filled with tears.

"Take the Crowns, all of them. I'll let them out; just don't hurt my baby boy or any officer here."

"Cap, you can't do that," Officer Dirk said.

"I most certainly can, and I will. Now me and my child are going back into the command center, and we'll let your crew go but not Jack. He stays with us. Got it?" Captain McBride said. "You got plans of killing him, you'll have to do that somewhere else, but not here and not on my watch."

"This big bitch got balls," Jake said with a hint of respect flashing across his face.

"Watch your mouth," Officer Dirk said. "She's my lady!" Captain McBride heard what he called her and smiled back at him. She actually blushed a little.

"What does the boy got?" Jake asked shaking the gun. "Why does he got no hair?"

"Cancer," Captain McBride said. "Douglas just had his last round of chemo at St. Jude's, and I had him brought here to protect him from vultures but worse came through the door!"

All of a sudden, the gang member with dreadlocks took a few steps toward Douglas pointing his gun.

"Stay away," Captain McBride said. In one swoop, Jake reached down and picked Douglas up right out of Captain McBride's arms.

"Let him go," I screamed. Rage boiling in the pit of my stomach caused me to shake.

"He isn't a part of this." Louigi came out of the employees' lounge.

"Now, you can have your gang members with no trouble from us. So, give us back Douglas and walk out of here right now."

The one with dreadlocks was clearly the leader because the others looked at him to see what he wanted them to do.

"As long as I got this boy, looks like we can get everything we want," Garrett said. "What's your name?"

"It's Douglas." He gave Jake a kick in the belly. He dropped Douglas then, and he landed square on his bottom.

"That little…" Jake withheld from cussing as all the Union gang members started to laugh.

"You just got your ass kicked by a baby." Sal leaned into him.

"You want Sally?"

"Shut up." Jake reached out to grab Douglas again, but he ran to Captain McBride and hid behind her leg.

"Now just go!" Douglas shouted.

"Not without our gang," he said, rubbing his belly.

"You want another kick?" Douglas asked. All the Union gang members started to laugh, even the ones in the cell.

"He's a tough little bugger," one said. Jack was watching from his cell. His uncle came forward and approached the Crown gang members without fear. All of a sudden, he started swinging, and the gang members pounced on him, kicking him and punching at his face.

"Let me out," Jack cried out.

"I can't do that," Captain McBride watched as they beat Jack's uncle senseless. He was motionless on the ground.

"Are you satisfied now?" Jake came forward, his dreadlocks falling in all directions.

"Let out our gang, and we'll only kill Jack's uncle today."

"I said I would let all your gang go. There's no reason to hurt anybody or threaten my little boy or Michael." Douglas came from around Captain McBride's leg and rushed over to Michael. He lay down on top of Michael before another punch was thrown.

"Stop hurting, Michael." Michael pushed him back.

"Stay away, Douglas! They'll hurt you, too."

Captain McBride realized Douglas was the only thing stopping them from beating Michael to death. Douglas stretched out on top of him, holding him tightly against his shirt sporting a train in case they went to punch Michael again. One of the other gang members held back the fist of the one with dreadlocks.

"I am not going to hit a kid," Garrett snipped.

"You looked like you were going to," Jake said. "He's got cancer. Leave him alone. Let's just get the crew and leave."

For a moment, the one with dreadlocks looked right at Captain McBride. "Today's your lucky day."

"It sure doesn't feel like a lucky day," Captain McBride said. "But I will agree to let out your Crown members if you leave and don't hurt anybody else. We just all want to go home in one piece."

"Protected by a baby. Guess your uncle's gonna live another day," Jake roared to Jack locked in a cell. "Only to die another."

CHAPTER 34

His eyes were locked on mine.

"So why don't you make things easy on us and you might live?" Jake said as his bright smile dimmed. Suddenly, another young man entered the room and stood next to the four.

"Dilly Willy," called one of the inmates from his cell.

"Good to see you." *So this was Dillon McHenry?* All I had to do was glance to our FBI Most Wanted list of juveniles to see his face. He was wanted in connection on four aggravated battery and burglary charges besides first-degree murder. Dillon McHenry noticed that I had glanced at the poster down the hall. He saw what I was looking at and moved closer to get a better view.

"I had thought you looked familiar," Officer Dirk said. How cocky! It was as if our two taser guns pointing at his chest weren't even there.

"You'd think they would have gotten a better angle," he said, moving one finger over his chin. "I prefer my left side over my right because of the knife scar." He then pointed to a large scar just under his eye. Officer Dirk took a step toward him and signaled me to get to the other side as he moved in. With three other guns pointed at them down the hall, Officer Dirk jumped at him. I swung the gangster around and put him into a very tight headlock. Immediately, I pushed his body around to face the other three. The one with the round face and small glasses roared,

"Let him go, man!" They had no choice but hold fire now or shoot McHenry in the front. McHenry seemed like he was the one calling the shots. Officer Dirk then raised his gun to Dillon McHenry's head.

A lump lodged in his throat as he warned, "I suggest you leave, or your leader is dead."

I don't know how we did it, but somehow, we managed to turn the tide and gain control of the situation. At least, I hoped we were on top now.

"Drop your weapons," Captain McBride roared, glancing around the room. Suddenly, a door from a cell swung open, but it wasn't one of the Crowns. Out stepped Jack the Mack. It was then I realized Jack had kicked down the door. He was so strong that he had actually bent the bars.

"Get back here," Michael ordered, shaking his head, and his smile faltered.

"Did you forget to lock his cell?" Officer Dirk asked me. I could hardly believe the words coming out of his mouth.

"Did he just break that?"

The five of the Crowns laughed until Jake commented, "You're dead, Jack!" Jack looked me in the eye and frowned.

"I'm gonna do you a favor," he grumbled. Jack the Mack grabbed my keys from my belt and started walking toward the cell of the Crowns.

"Dilly Willy isn't their leader; Jake Marshall killed about twelve kids in my neighborhood over drugs."

"Sixteen," Jake shouted as his face flushed.

"The punk you have is only a newbie, and they would kill him for their Crown brothers who are their dealers."

An inmate sniffed and took a step out of his cell the moment Jack had unlocked it. He stared us down and then said, "You cops never learn." Down the hallway, Jack headed toward all the members of the Crowns. He unlocked their cells, so now instead of facing five, we were facing ten.

"You leave here. All of you will be hunted down like dogs," Captain McBride said with raised eyebrows. The ten of them headed toward the front door. Just as they passed Captain McBride, Jake turned his head and stared at Ms. McBride. He went silent for a moment, then, "Woof," he said. Then when the ten of them stood at the door, they stopped. They had hurried only to discover that they had been stopped by not the police outside but a wall of red-eyed vultures hovering above.

CHAPTER 35

ake paused only for a moment. The expression on his face was rage mixed with fear.

"They are just birds," he said.

Sal was the first to say with intensity in his darkened eyes, "I've got your back, M."

"Me too," stammered Garrett. The ten walked out in the center heading to a van that was running in the parking lot. In front was a woman with long, dark hair and light features. Her tank top was twisted in front to further show her large bosom. I recognized her at once as Marla, Jack's ex-girlfriend. A vulture flew over and landed directly on top of the front passenger's window. Marla screamed, but it just sat there staring down at her. Quickly, she rolled up the window.

"Did you see that?" Sal asked Jake as I walked out into the parking lot behind him. He tempered his hard question with a frown. Jake whirled around, pointing his gun with widening eyes.

"You think you gonna stop us?" he asked me.

"Looks like I'm not your biggest problem at the moment," I said, my eyes turning to the row of vultures now perched on the top of the van.

"Stay back," said Captain McBride as I felt her hand on my shoulder. The urgency raised in her voice, "Stay back!"

"That would be the easy way," I admitted with a poisonous glare.

"They ain't worth risking your life," Captain McBride blinked and said through gritted teeth.

"That's not for me to judge." I took another step out and clicked my taser gun.

"She won't shoot us," Garrett mumbled. The group grumbling petered out for a moment.

"Open the van door, Marla," yelled Jake. "Then we'll all run for it."

"I say we walk real slow instead," grimaced Sal as he cleared his throat.

"They are sizing us up." Garrett gulped.

"Look at that one." Jake glanced over to where Dillion was pointing. The vulture to the right sitting on top of a light pole had blood pouring from its beak. "That could be from its last meal."

"All right, on the count of three, we run for the van. Everyone loaded?"

"I wouldn't do that," I warned as my face flushed with fear. "They are attracted to action. You best take Sal's advice and go slow."

"Shut up, Pig," said Jake with desperation in his voice.

"Okay." I smirked; then I raised my taser. "You're right; I am not going to kill any of you, but I will kill those vultures."

"One…" yelled Jake. The second he did, all the vulture turned their heads in unison staring directly at him.

"Holy…crap! Did you see that?" Garrett gasped, and his gaze lingered on the birds. "They're gonna kill us. They'll bite our peckers off."

"Shut up," ordered Jake, then said to Marla. "You ready, sister?"

Jack warned from the doorway, "Don't, Marla!" Marla moved to the door and opened it just a crack. A vulture leaped from the passenger-side window to directly above the van's door. Marla screamed as tears began to roll down her cheeks.

"Don't be scared," Jake said, shaking his head.

"Two!" The ten men got closer together, leaning forward as if to run, and then the last number came out of the mouth of Jake.

"Three." It wouldn't be the ten men who moved, however. That would be the vultures who flew. More vultures began to fly above the ten Crown young men. The Crowns started to scream. As the door of the van opened, a vulture flew in and began to attack Marla, who had just gotten in the driver's seat. I started to shoot. One vulture dropped to the ground, but instead of scaring the others away, more came. Dozens of them flew down from the trees blackening the sky with the giant creatures. Captain McBride grabbed me and pulled me back in just as a vulture began to head toward the door of the facility.

"We can't let them get in!"

"They'll all die out there," I said.

"It's too late." Ms. McBride grabbed me and forced me to stare out of the window. Hardly believing my eyes, I witnessed what was left of the ten Crown men and Marla with the running van—nothing but blood and pieces scattered. The birds had pulled them apart.

"They did this to themselves," Captain McBride said. "We warned them. They were just too cocky to realize that you can't beat Mother Nature!"

"This isn't Mother Nature." I gasped. "It's unnatural!"

Captain McBride grabbed my shoulders tightly. "You did what you could for them. Now I need to call Donald, that general manager of the Wildlife Commission. We need to find out what we are dealing with and what the hell has gotten into these vultures. It's got to be some kind of flu or virus that has driven them crazy."

Officer Dirk stepped to my side. "Looks like they do know how to clean up after all." Captain McBride glared at him.

"We had a duty to protect them, criminals or not. Camp was right, but there was nothing any of us could do. They decided to try a prison break in the middle of some kind of end-of-the-world stuff."

"I might have agreed with you if they hadn't threatened Douglas," Officer Dirk said. I ran into the facility and headed to where I had last seen Louigi. He was still standing there motionless.

"They killed them all."

"Yes," I gulped. "But we are no longer under attack."

"I saw the birds coming," Jack said. "That's the only reason I let those Crowns out of the cell. They were too dumb not to realize that the vultures were more likely to kill them than any of you."

"Did you kick down your cell door?" I asked Jack. Jack was picking up his uncle then and carrying him to lay in the employees' lounge.

"The lounge is still safe," I remembered.

"Get the fire doors in front of the cell wing," Captain McBride ordered. "Everyone else, go into the employees' lounge. We've still got a job to do."

I rushed to the fire doors and said to the inmates, "You all are safe in here. So, remain calm, and we'll be back as soon as we can."

"Don't leave us," one inmate begged.

"What happened?" another asked.

"Did the birds get them?" questioned another.

"Yes," I replied, "but so far, they are staying outside. We are going to lock these doors, and you will all be safe. We're calling the police for back up. Just remain calm."

"Remain calm?" one snipped. "There are killer birds out there strong enough to take down Jake and the Crown gang."

Captain McBride must have heard him because she reiterated what I said. "You all are to stay here until reinforcements arrive. We will be transporting you to another facility as soon as we know it is safe." With that, she slammed the fire doors, and I locked it.

"They shouldn't be in there alone without an officer," I said. Captain McBride shook her head.

"I know, but we need to stay safe, too." She headed down the hall, and I trailed after her. As I walked toward the employees' lounge, I saw that the black birds were starting to enter through the door that had collapsed.

"Hurry!" Captain McBride opened the door, and we entered. Inside I saw the other officers, Louigi, Douglas, and Michael, who was lying on the sofa.

"Are they all dead?" Michael rolled over and asked.

"Yes," Captain McBride answered.

"They took out the Crown gang who were all armed," Jack said.

"You should be back in your cell," Captain McBride snipped at him.

"Did you see what he did to his cell?" I asked her.

"One kick, and the door flew off its hinges."

"My dad taught me what to do to get out of a cell," Jack said. "For the record, I could have done that anytime I was here. I only did it to free the Crowns so no one would be killed but them. I don't think they would have left without their gang members. The Crowns may be a lot of things, but they are loyal to one another."

Michael smiled. "You saved us all."

"But not them," Jack said.

"I knew that the birds would kill them and let them out anyway. It was the only way." Captain McBride understood.

"They weren't going without their gang."

"I thought the front door was bulletproof," Officer Dirk said.

"It was taken down by an AK47," Captain McBride said. "Good thing it ran out of bullets or who knows what would have happened."

"So that's how it was done," I said, then turned to Jack.

"Thanks for letting the Crowns out of their cells. None of us could have done that and still had a conscience."

"I have to live with the fact, though, that I let them out knowing that they might be killed by what was waiting outside."

"They are attracted to noise," Louigi said, then spoke to Jack. "I noticed that when I was in the cabin. Those gunshots attracted them. It's not your fault."

"This is Jack," I introduced him to Louigi.

"Jack, this is my husband Louigi."

"So, you're the lucky man?" Jack said.

"You've got quite a brave officer. Actually, all of you are brave to face the Crowns fully armed and live."

"We didn't ask for this," Captain McBride said. "Now we're the ones who will have to explain how about five of our inmates escaped and were killed by a bunch of vultures."

"I think the public will understand," I said.

"No, they won't." Captain McBride shook her head no. "No explanation is going to satisfy their parents. All these people died on our watch, vultures or not."

"This is just the thing that will get this facility closed," Officer Dirk said.

"And all of us might lose our jobs," Captain McBride added. "If it comes to that, I will take the fall for the whole thing."

"You most certainly will not," Jack interrupted. "I broke down the door and let them out while you all were held at gunpoint. No one is to blame for what happened but those damn birds. None of us."

"They were the ones who walked out of this facility into a mess. They saw the birds on the van and even ordered Marla to go over there to open the door. That was sending her to her death, and Jake knew it. I hate that guy with a passion, but that was even a new low for him. They knew that they either get outta here or face jail time themselves."

"You are right about that," I said.

"We need to stop talking about what happened in front of Douglas." Officer Dirk pointed down at the little boy standing beside Michael. Michael's face was beaten and bloody and now starting to swell.

"We got a medic kit in here," Captain McBride said. "It's in the cabinet right above the vending machine."

Officer Dirk hurried to the kit and opened it. Inside were antibiotic ointment and bandages; Officer Dirk dumped the contents above Michael. "We'll do what we can. The Cokes are cold so we can use those as ice."

"Thank you all for helping my uncle," Jack said, bending down to assist Officer Dirk.

"Thank you," I said. "If it wasn't for you, we'd all still be facing guns."

"You saved us," Officer Dirk said.

"All of us." Douglas reached up and held Michael's hand as Officer Dirk began to clean his wounds.

"You are so precious," Michael said to him, then turned to Captain McBride. "He is like an angel."

CHAPTER 36

All dead. At least that is what I had thought. It wasn't until we had heard her screams did, we realize that Marla had somehow survived in the van. We heard her screaming, "Open up," while banging on the employees' lounge door. Jack immediately rushed for the door to let her in, but several vultures swooped down on her. She fell backwards onto the floor. Not hesitating, Jack stepped out into the hallway to try to fight the birds off of her. I remembered how she had betrayed him by not telling him that she was a Crown, yet despite their history, Jack risked his life to save her. He punched the vultures off of her as others flew at him. It took him a few seconds, with lots of birds getting punched, before he was able to grab one of her legs and pull her inside, then shut the employees' lounge door. She was covered in cuts and scratches. Marla would never be the same, no longer the perfect beauty she once had been.

"Thank you, Jack." Marla grabbed him. Love brightening her eyes. Gratitude shined across her face with the glow of thankfulness.

"You saved my life!" She was smeared in blood.

"Let's get you bandaged up. You think we got enough?" Jack asked Officer Dirk.

"There's another kit in the cabinet." Officer Dirk turned to get Captain McBride with a withering glance.

"You better lend them a hand," Captain McBride said to me as she pushed the dark hair out of her eyes.

"I've got this," Officer Dirk grabbed another emergency kit and returned to begin bandaging Marla.

"This is madness. We aren't trained to fight off flying monsters," Captain McBride added. I ignored her command to help Marla and went to peek out the doorway. I wanted to know just how many of them were out there and if any had managed to smash the fire door leading to the inmates. All I could see were grey brick walls and a flashing light from a dangling EXIT sign.

"You are putting us all at risk," I heard from Captain McBride as she winced at the bitterness of her words.

"Close and lock that thing up." That's when I heard something that sounded like the swooshing of giant wings. Perhaps another time I would have thought of angels hearing such a noise, but this wasn't an angel, unless one that had come straight out of hell. In an instant, I glanced at the largest vulture I had ever seen. The one I had just hit with my taser was now about two feet behind me, in front of the flapping, giant wings. It was flying toward the fire doors down the hallway where the inmates were.

"They are going for the cells," I announced with fear flared in my eyes. "Dirk, we got to protect the kids."

"They are behind bars," Officer Dirk reminded.

"Close the door." "They won't be able to get through that door," Captain McBride reminded. "Now shut our door before one gets in here!"

I shut the door to the lounge, reluctantly, but in truth I knew that such a large vulture might be able to break that lock. Perhaps the inmates were safe behind the bars as long as they stayed far enough away from where the birds could get them.

"I'm so sorry, Jack," Marla whispered, hoarsely. He was removing the bloody hair from out of her face.

"We don't need to talk about this now."

"I love you. That wasn't a lie," she muttered. "I always did. I couldn't tell you I was a Crown. I knew you would reject me."

"You probably tried to get me to Mexico for the Crowns," Jack said, studying her face. "It all was a lie to get me to leave so they could take over."

"That's not true," Marla said, holding his hand. "You're right; I did want us to go with your father but not for that reason. I wanted us to be together, forever, and I knew that was the only way we could be. The Crowns and the Union would never let our relationship continue. The Crowns knew how I felt about you and were willing to let me go."

"Is it a trap?" Jack asked her. He was silent for a time.

"Is my father in danger in Mexico?"

"No," Marla told him. "They just wanted him gone to run the city. He can start a new life without the Union or living in a cell. I wanted what was best for you and him. It was never about hurting either one of you. I love you. If you don't believe anything else, believe that. I risked everything so that you would have that chance. You didn't want to go. I understand that now."

Just then a loud crashing noise sounded. It was the fire doors, and I knew it. That giant bird was banging into it to break it down. I slowly cracked the door again to see my fears realized. Next to the fire safety door was a pile of vultures that had just hit it with everything they got. They were all trying to get down the hallway where the inmates were. Suddenly, I saw a split in the door, and one of the vultures managed to slip into the hallway. One was enough to send chills down my spine. Where had it gone to eat one of the inmates? They were my responsibility. Could I subdue it before it killed one of our inmates?

CHAPTER 37

Screams resounded down the hallway as the inmates yelled at one another that the vultures were now inside the hallway. Louigi handed me a nail gun. There were a few of these in that cabinet. He tossed Officer Dirk another one. Officer Dirk smiled.

"This will do. You ready, Camp?"

"This is the last one," Louigi said staring back at me.

"You stay here," I said. "Protect everyone here with that."

"I am going with you." Louigi stepped forward. "I can help."

"He can take the back," Officer Dirk said. His voice sounded more alert.

"Okay, I got the front, and you hold up above," I said.

"We go together."

"I will help too." Jack had a nail gun on his hand. A smile teased the corners of his mouth. "It was in the cabinet next to yours."

"Don't rush," Louigi said with an intense look in his eyes.

"Jack, they hold about twenty nails each."

There was no sight of the bird as I slowly opened the door, but there was a smell of blood and bird feathers.

"Be careful and watch your backs." Captain McBride hurried to the door to close it after we all stepped through. We made an X with our bodies. Every step we moved as a team, with our nail guns aimed to shoot at any bird. All the birds had climbed into the hole in the fire doors and were now attacking the inmates down the hallway. They were pecking at them through the bars. When we reached the doors, Officer Dirk pulled the latch and then yanked open the door. What we found inside was shocking. The birds had managed to squeeze themselves into several of the cells. All the inmates were against the walls. Some were holding pillows as if to beat them back with it.

"Can you let us out now?" one asked with a panicking expression on his face. Officer Dirk moved to the emergency latch on the wall and punched in his code. All of the cell doors opened at once. With our nail guns aimed, I shouted orders.

"All of you get out of the cells, run down the hall to the employees' lounge and wait there. Got it."

"I'm not moving," another replied. "They're gonna eat me."

"Stay calm," Officer Dirk yelled.

"They are attracted to movement."

"And you want us to run?" said one clutching his pillow.

"It's coming for me!"

A black vulture was coming forward toward him very slowly, watching his every move.

"Should I kick it?" another asked with a questioning look.

"Okay, I want you all to run when I say go," I said with my adrenaline tingling my nerves.

"Race down the hall to the employees' lounge and wait for us."

"Ready?" I looked down the hall. I looked in every cell and saw the fear on their faces.

"You can do this! We got weapons, so if they come after you, we'll kill them." Officer Dirk put his hand on Louigi's shoulder. He hesitated, then nodded.

"Get ready."

"We got this," Jack said. His big eyes widening.

"Go!" I screamed, and like an army, the kids ran through their doors and down the hall beside us. A few of the vultures snapped their beaks at the running youth, but surprisingly, none were harmed. Suddenly, as if in sync, the birds began to hiss and spread their wings. I'd never heard anything more terrifying in my life. It was worse than any snake. It was as if the devil himself hissed at us noisily. I heard the employees' lounge door open and Captain McBride order them to stand in line at the door. After that, the door slammed.

"Okay." I shrugged.

"We're going backwards very slowly. Got it?" I took a step back, my nail gun pointed outward. Jack and Louigi were right behind me, and Officer Dirk was covering the back. We took several more steps toward the employee's lounge. The big one, the one who had broken the door. Where had it gone? Where could it have gone? Officer Dirk stopped and glared at me wearily.

"The kids are safe. Where is the giant one?"

"He's the least of our worries." I said; then I turned to Jack behind me.

"Did you see where the big one went?"

With one finger, he pointed up. It was then that I looked above and saw an enormous hole in the ceiling. It had knocked one of the ceiling tiles loose and had gone into the ductwork. At the edge of the gaping hole were claw marks.

"All of a sudden it must have gone upward." Officer Dirk said.

"Let's keep moving."

Then I heard it. Up above our heads, scratching. It was then I realized that this bird could drop into the employees' lounge. The other vultures were forming a line in the center of the cells. Slowly, they were coming towards us as we backed away. Catching my breath, I glanced up.

"We have a vulture in the ceiling," said Officer Dirk.

"Can he get to the employees' lounge through the vents?"

"Yes," I answered.

"Can you see the big one up there?" Jack asked.

"I don't see it."

"Me either." Louigi gasped.

"But keep moving. The rest are coming after us."

"Just stick close to me," I said. The group continued to back up as the line of vultures grew and moved toward them. They flapped their wings and continued to hiss. Every once in awhile, one would jump forward, but all four of us would point our nail guns at it. A scratching noise came directly from above us.

"It's up there." "Right above us," Jack said, moving the nail gun to point above his head. Another bang came from above.

"That sounded farther away," I realized.

"From the command center." Suddenly, loud, masculine screams could be heard around the corner. All of us rushed down the hallway and made a turn. On the floor was a police officer.

"Officer down," I called into my handset. He moved and rolled over.

"It was so fast." I couldn't believe how calm he seemed with so much blood loss and a scratch across his face that nearly took out an eyeball. Over the handset came a call that an ambulance was on its way.

"You are going to be just fine, Officer."

"It's Officer Mason Ray," he said, his voice cracking. "I got a wife and two kids, and I never thought if I'd go it would be because of a stupid bird."

"Not stupid," Officer Dirk said.

"Come with us to the employees' lounge."

"I don't think so," said Officer Ray. "It got me pretty good." Slowly, he showed us his back, and through the torn flesh, I could see the back of his ribs.

"Oh, that." Officer Dirk's eyes began to well. "That's just a flesh wound."

"Tell my kids I love them," he said.

"You're not going anywhere." I hoped.

"Now, Louigi and Jack, you help him up; we are going to go to the employees' lounge." I looked over and saw Captain McBride ready to open the door.

"I am a rookie. I just started six months ago when I moved from California. I thought that this would be an easy job, with all the elderly living here. Boy was I wrong! I got the call that the facility was under attack and came as fast as I can. There's more coming." I glanced over at Officer Dirk. He could barely look at the man on the ground. Quickly, he bent down and began to cover the hole in the man's back with his shirt. Louigi didn't flinch at the open wound but immediately said,

"Let's keep his head up."

"You are doing good," I said to him.

"This is nothing compared to seeing cow parts," he said.

"But let's get to the employees' lounge now." I nodded.

"Jack and Louigi, you two lift him up and carry him if need be. Then we'll head straight to the lounge."

"Do I look like something a butcher cut up?" the officer asked me.

"No way," Officer Dirk said. Louigi grimaced.

"I'm sorry, Officer. I didn't mean it like that."

Sirens blared coming down the street. They were loud but not loud enough to drown out the hissing noises coming from the vultures.

"Told you they were coming," the officer said weakly. "I asked for an ambulance."

"Good thinking," I said. Another squawk came from above. This one was the loudest noise I had ever heard come from a bird. It seemed to come directly from above us.

"It's coming back to finish the job," Officer Ray said.

"We won't let him," my husband said.

"No, we have your…"

"Were you going to say back…?" My husband gave me a look. The ceiling above us came down, and the vulture lunged at us with his claws out. Louigi immediately fired his nail gun, and a nail shot from the gun into the center of the vulture's chest, directly into its heart. It fell the rest of the way, in between us, dead and motionless.

"You got him," Jack said. Louigi and Jack helped the wounded officer back to his feet. He was growing paler by the moment. Just then police cars pulled into the JDC parking lot. I saw about six Officers heading our way with guns pointed. They passed the bloody mess outside by the Crown's van and hurried in. It didn't take them long to see the row of vultures coming towards us.

"The safest place is in the employees' lounge," I called out.

Captain McBride waved to the officers.

"The rest of us are in here."

One officer asked, "You okay, Ray?"

"Not good," the officer replied. "That you, Bernie?"

"Yes, it's me, Ray. The hell of a day you're having. An ambulance is on its way," came a reply from another officer who looked middle-aged. His gun was drawn toward the row of vultures coming toward us ever so slowly.

"We need to get Ray inside the lounge," I said to the one who replied to Bernie.

"You two got Ray?" Bernie asked Louigi.

"We are going to run for it," Louigi said.

"Those nail guns work?" Bernie questioned.

"I got one," Jack pulled Officer Ray further to his feet.

"Okay, all of us need to go toward that room." I pointed to the lounge.

"You ready, Cap?"

"Ready," she replied.

"Now!" I roared, and the four of us and the officers followed. All of a sudden, the birds took flight. I tried to shoot them, but they were so fast. By the time we reached the lounge, there were a few vultures dead on the floor but still just as many flapping their wings coming our way. The door to the lounge opened, and we carried Officer Ray in with us. Michael was now on his feet, so Louigi and Jack carried Officer Ray to the sofa. Just as the door was about to shut, a vulture tried to get in. Captain McBride closed the door on its head and wing, but that didn't kill it. Its eyes were crazed as it tried to snap at the captain's fingers. Finally, she shoved the head back and managed to close the door, keeping the birds out and all of the humans trapped inside the employees' lounge.

"We got towels?" I asked the captain.

"Officer Ray's losing a lot of blood."

"Yes." Captain McBride hurried to a bottom cabinet next to the water fountain.

"How long before the ambulance is here?"

Bernie shook the captain's hand.

"You managed to keep all these kids safe."

"All but the Crowns by the van," Captain McBride said.

"Great job, Captain," Officer Bernie finished shaking her hand.

"Ambulance is on his way. Looks like that one could use a ride to the hospital, too. Is he the only one injured?"

"That's still alive," Captain McBride said.

CHAPTER 38

After the ambulance drove right to the building with the siren running, the noise seemed to scare the vultures back. Two EMTs rushed in carrying their equipment. Captain McBride quickly shut the door after their arrival. The noise seemed to scare the birds. Officer Ray had lost a lot of blood, but I had hoped that they would get him to the hospital in time to save his life. These two EMTs quickly patched him up, carried him on a stretcher, and wheeled him back into the ambulance. They took Michael with him, and although I could tell that Jack wanted to go with his uncle, he fell in line with the other inmates and put down the nail gun.

"Thanks," I whispered to Jack. Scratching noises could be heard overhead.

"I think you should rethink keeping your nail gun." Louigi turned to me with a penetrating gaze.

"More went up that hole and are crawling all through the ducts?"

Captain McBride reached down for Jack's nail gun and handed it back to him. "You better keep this. You got the big one."

"It was nothing." Jack's lips turned into a crooked smile.

"I saw it happen," Captain McBride said with gladness radiating in her expression. "It came down out of the hole in the ceiling. It happened very fast, faster than I could have imagined it could. Apparently, this disease improved their strength and ability to fly. You got him straight in the heart though."

"The EMTs called ahead. Let's hope they have Officer Ray's blood type at the hospital. The skin was deeply cut, but it should be stitched back in place. From what I saw, the organs are intact. So, he'll probably live." Bernie forced himself to focus and pinched the bridge of his nose.

"That's good to hear, Captain," McBride said. "That doesn't solve the problem that now we have a vulture in the ceiling. I do have an idea, though."

"What's that?"

Captain McBride kicked in the glass of the vending machine. "Let's get the food and throw it in the center of the hall. When they all go for it, we'll..."

"Remember last week when we went fishing, Dirk?" Captain McBride asked. The fact that they had gone fishing was news to me. I found it odd that my partner hadn't admitted to me that they did. It seemed almost betrayal that he hadn't told me, and I immediately wondered why.

"I just happened to run into her at the bridge." Officer Dirk leaned over to me. A lingering look from the captain seemed to bolster his courage. "I saw her fishing and stopped to see if she caught anything."

"You had a net," Captain McBride said.

"Yes, I toss a net off my boat occasionally."

"It was in the back of your truck. I remember you offered it to me in case I wanted to toss it into the river since I hadn't caught anything all afternoon," Captain McBride reminded. "We could bait them with food and then toss the net on these birds." Louigi's eyes widened.

"That's perfect! That would work!"

"Where's the net?" Officer Bernie asked Dirk.

"It's in the back of my truck in the parking lot." Officer Dirk moved to a locker at the end of the lounge. Captain McBride heard more scratches above.

"Then let's not waste any time in getting it and trapping all these birds. Not the time to go out with the family,"

Officer Dirk said. "Yes, Captain, I do have that net in the back of my truck, which is parked now just outside the garage with those vultures in our way."

"We can't let any more in the ceiling get in here," I said. The stress was palpable. My heart was hammering. Scratching was heard just above our heads.

"Do you think it hears us?" Officer Dirk said with his breath sounding in my ears.

"It almost seems to be listening." It was then that I realized how quiet the facility was. Every single juvenile and all the officers on the monitors were looking up and silent as if waiting to see who this vulture's next victim would be.

"I like your plan, Captain," Officer Dirk said then asked in a querulous voice. "But I don't see how we can make that happen without more weapons."

Captain McBride cracked open the door and showed Officer Bernie where Dirk's pick-up truck was in the parking lot. It was parked in the spot right next to the parking garage, the closest, fastest place to run to get away had it not been for the ambulance leaving.

"See how the vans are all on the right side? It may be possible to sneak behind them and the vultures do not notice until you get to the door. I can open the door from here, and then you could run out to the truck," Officer Bernie snapped.

Captain McBride shook her head no. "Officer Dirk isn't going to even attempt that. There must be a better way to get to that truck than by foot."

"Climbing to the ceiling is out," Louigi said.

"We'd be lunch for the rest of them. No, we need to figure out a way to trap them all without putting any more of us at risk. We know now what just one can do."

"I can get it," Jack pointed out.

"I can run faster than any of you. I'll do it."

"No." But before I realized it, Jack sped through the employees' lounge door. He went alone through the vultures. He moved so fast, I could barely believe my eyes. He ran to the truck just as the birds took flight. With one swoop, he picked up the net and ran back. This time, he had to fire the nail gun to stop two of them from clawing him. He shot them dead right in the heart as he had the largest one. In less than thirty seconds, he had run outside, grabbed the giant fishing net, and returned.

"Oh, like that, is it?" Captain McBride smiled at him.

"I got it." Jack held it up.

"Are you crazy?" I asked him.

"Just fast," Jack said.

"No shit," Officer Bernie added.

"Okay," Captain McBride said.

"So, we'll toss out all this food, wait until they are all in the middle, and then toss this net on them. That should keep them in one place and stop them from flying."

"Sounds like a great plan," Louigi agreed. That's when we started opening bags of nachos and candy bars and tossing them into the hallway. Raw meat was taken out of the fridge and thrown on top the pile. Before long, all of the vultures, even the ones above in the ceiling, flew down through the holes and were eating our food. Officer Dirk took the net and whirled it over his head. In a big swoop, while the vultures were all distracted with the food, he covered them in the net. The weight of the net seemed to hold them down.

"Got them," Officer Dirk said. With that, he quickly moved into the hall and began tying the net down to the furniture in the room. The birds were all trapped inside the net and it was as safe as it could be for us to leave the Employee Lounge.

"All right," Captain McBride snapped. "I want all inmates to go to the garage and load in the biggest van, on the bus. We're taking you all upstate. Officer Dirk and Camp will drive you. The rest of us are getting in our cars and going home."

"I'm going with my wife," Louigi said.

"Fine, this once," Captain McBride said.

"We'll give the van a police escort," Bernie said. The inmates got up to walk out the door. The vultures snapped at them, but they were caught in the nets. We looked all around, but no others attempted to attack as we approached the biggest van, which was nearly a bus. All the inmates entered the bus; we didn't bother cuffing them. They all behaved themselves as they loaded into the bus to go to the JDC upstate. In fact, instead of any complaints from them, some of them gave us fist bumps as they walked past. A couple nodded and another saluted Officer Bernie. It made me feel good that all of them were doing the right thing and not giving us trouble when it would have been very easy to escape. They loaded the bus, and I sat in the passenger's seat while Officer Dirk sat behind the wheel. He moved the mirror to see that all the inmates had been seated. It was then I noticed that our most famous inmate was missing.

"Where's Jack?" I asked Officer Dirk. Jack was helping Marla to the bus. He had his arm around her. There were scratches down her face, but they still looked happy.

"Glad you could join us," I said to Jack as he helped Marla up the stairs and down a few rows to take an empty seat. "However, you are not one of our inmates, Marla. You don't have to come with us."

"She should go to the hospital and have her face stitched up," Officer Dirk said.

"I am going for a ride, and then I'll go to the hospital," Marla said.

"I am making sure that Jack is fine."

"You don't have to worry about him." I laughed.

"That's one thing I am sure of; Jack can take care of himself." Jack handed me the nail gun.

"Here, I won't be needing this any longer." I took the nail gun away from him and put it in the glove box.

"You really mind, Marla, going with us for a ride?"

Seeing how happy they were to be together, "It's the least we can do after all you did to help us," I added.

"I just want to be with my lady a little longer," he said. She blushed as he sat down beside her.

"So, you've decided to forgive me?'

"We've got lots to work on, and I got to get freed of my charges."

"Don't worry about that." Captain McBride stuck her head into the bus. "I'll take care of that stealing the car. You raised money for my boy's hospital, killed the biggest vulture, and helped us trap the rest. I think your stealing a car can be forgiven."

"That's funny," Jack said. "I didn't actually steal that car. The owner told me to take it for a ride. He wasn't even the one who reported it."

"What?" Captain McBride said.

"It's true." Marla smiled. "The Crowns set up the whole thing so he would miss the boxing match. Jack is actually innocent." Officer Dirk glanced over at me not surprised.

"So, you're here because of a gang war, not because of a missing car."

"It wasn't missing at all," Jack said. "I'm sure now that the Crowns are mostly dead, the owners will come forward with the truth."

"Then the charges should be dropped," I said. "If the car wasn't stolen, you'll be set free as soon as the judge hears all this."

"I hope so," Jack said. "That way I can spend time with my baby."

"I'm still your baby." Marla's eyes filled with tears. "After all that I did?"

"Did you mean what you said?" Jack asked her. "Do you really love me, Marla?"

"I do." Marla smiled. "But can you love me now that I will probably be all scarred up?"

"What scars?" Jack kissed her lips.

"Well, I'll be darn," Captain McBride said.

"Looks like things are looking up after all. These two are in love."

"I'll be sure to invite you all to our wedding." Jack winked.

"Douglas can be our ringbearer."

"If his cancer is truly gone, you can count on that."

"Good." Marla smiled. "I wouldn't want anyone else to be."

"All right, buckle up," Officer Dirk said; then he winked at Captain McBride.

"I'm hoping that won't be the only wedding." Captain McBride smiled and shut the bus door. My heart was elated. I felt Louigi's hand began rubbing my neck. I glanced over to see him sitting behind me, and all the inmates began to clap. I had never felt so blessed in all my life to have such a strong, loving husband and such great friends. Suddenly, Louigi moved his head and kissed me on the lips. Marla and Jack began kissing as well. The clapping didn't end for quite some time, because those kisses lasted a very, very long time.

CHAPTER 39

The bus was barreling down the highway when a loud thud on the roof of the bus imparted. Then came another.

"What is that?" Jack asked me with a slight twist of the lips.

"I don't know," I answered, peering through the bus windows looking up. I spotted a vulture about a hundred yards flying beside the bus. It frightened me that he could keep up with a vehicle going nearly seventy miles an hour.

"How many of them are out there?" Officer Dirk asked me. His face contorted with a hint of fear. I looked out but saw only one. Then another thump hit the bus roof, but this time, a vulture rolled down the windshield to fall under the tire.

"It's dead." Officer Dirk drew my attention toward the winged, motionless creature. My eyes glanced back to the one flying, and it dropped to the ground.

"That one just died, too."

"What's happening to them?" Jack looked up and saw another vulture as it dropped right out of the sky. Another vulture hit the roof, and Officer Dirk slowed the van down to a stop right in the middle of the highway.

"Why did you stop?" I asked him with my gut churning.

"Look ahead." He pointed, his eyes widening. I could barely believe my eyes. For the next mile in front of the bus lay dead vultures all over the highway like hundreds of motionless roadkill. The ones still that could fly were also dropping dead, one after another.

"They're all dying." Jack gasped through gritted teeth.

"It sure looks that way." Officer Dirk smiled. He then restarted the bus and continued down the highway. We rolled over the dead birds. The ride wasn't pleasant, especially hearing the thud sounds every time a bird corpse went underneath the tires. Our roof continued to be hit by dying birds falling out of the sky. Once we got to the JDC upstate, the bus rolled into the parking lot. Dead vultures lay scattered there. Several corrections officers met the bus. Officer Dirk opened the door; I stood.

"All right, we're going to line up into their facility where you will be checked in and assigned a new cell." I leaned over to Marla. "You're free to stay, and we'll give you a ride back home."

"Thank you," she said, swallowing hard. "Officer Camp."

"My name's Laura," I said with brightening eyes.

"You can call me Laura."

One by one, the inmates formed a perfect line in front of the JDC officers. Marla continued to sit in her seat. When everyone else had left, Jack gave her one last kiss on the lips and left her side.

"I love you, Jack," Marla said, whispered as he descended the stairs and stepped to the end of the line.

"You know, we're going to be written up for not having them in cuffs," Officer Dirk said to me. One of the officers approached the bus.

"You Camp and Dirk?"

"I'm Dirk," Officer Dirk said to the stranger in uniform.

"I'm Camp."

"Good job." He saluted. "We'll take it from here."

"Thanks," I said as we saluted him back, and my vision suddenly blurred with tears.

"By the way, we got word from animal control that the disease was actually some form of weird parasite altered by Space Shuttle radiation which was stolen from the Space United building in a bottle. The bottle broke and the gas deformed the parasite and then they spread like a virus among the vultures. They discovered the parasite on one of the dead ones. It only attacks the vultures through their nostrils. This parasite enters their brains and makes them go crazy. It attacks their frontal lobe, the part that tells them that they are full, so they don't have any control of their hunger. The parasite continues to eat their brain until they die."

"So that's why they all are dying?' I said, watching more vultures drop from the sky.

"Yes, looks like the situation is going to take care of itself after all." Officer Dirk restarted the bus, which hosted a roof full of dead vultures. As he turned, a few fell to the ground. We rolled over more to approach the highway. I had no idea so many vultures lived in Florida.

"Thank God it's going to be over soon," I said, shaking my head.

"Let's hope forever." Officer Dirk smiled.

"I never want to see a vulture ever again."

"Me either," Marla said.

"All those people died because of a stupid parasite that seemed to eat vulture brains. Sounds like something straight out of a horror movie."

"I wouldn't have believed it if someone told me that this could even happen," Officer Dirk announced as the bus returned to the highway. More birds were on the road now; hundreds, maybe thousands were on the ground as far as the eye could see. I looked out above, and for the first time in an hour, I didn't see any more vultures in the sky.

"It's getting clear out."

"Finally," Louigi said to me.

"We can finally believe there is an end to all this."

The sun was beginning to set again. I was so tired. It felt like forever since I slept. Tonight, I would be able to go home again. Home to my parents getting along and my dog, Doofus.

"Maybe we should all take a nap," Louigi said, closing his eyes to the beautiful sunset, which was casting rays on all of the dead birds. The bus bumped over another one and another.

"Sorry, this won't be a smooth ride back," Officer Dirk said to Louigi.

"That's okay," Louigi said.

"Tonight, I am going to sleep in my own bed."

"Oh, I think that sounds like a very good idea." I reached out, and he grabbed my hand to hold.

"I hope your parents didn't kill each other," he laughed.

"They really don't get along," Officer Dirk recalled.

"Your house may have turned into a war zone."

We returned to the facility, and Louigi got into my car. The roads were covered with dead vultures all the way home. Louigi opened my door for me and wrapped his arm around me as we went to the door. Doofus began to bark as we walked in to find my parents sitting next to one another on the sofa, my father's arm lovingly around her. The look on their faces, the tears that came, and then the hugs. I will never be able to forget what it felt like to almost lose everything and then suddenly realize you still have it all.

CHAPTER 40

oofus was dressed in a doggie black and white tuxedo with a pink corsage tied to his collar. He looked cute running around the backyard greeting guests at the backyard wedding. Underneath the palm trees was a white gazebo set up with white and pink roses cascading from flower boxes. White chairs were set up in back of it as guests took their seats waiting for the wedding to begin. The Wedding March began to be performed by members of the Space Coast Symphony Orchestra conducted by Aaron Collins. I knew that was my clue to begin walking in front of Captain McBride. Douglas was dressed up in a little tuxedo with a pink rose in his lapel. I gave a smile looking down at him. All of this fancy dressing was for Captain McBride as she married my partner, Officer Dirk. The patio doors of my house opened, and out came Captain McBride in a long, white wedding gown. Her hair was up and covered in white pearls, which matched her earrings and necklace. I'd never seen the captain in a dress before, and she looked gorgeous with makeup, even long eye lashes, her radiant beauty shone more than her dress and hairstyle. Actually, her beauty came from more than her dress and hairstyle. She was glowing. She walked slowly behind Douglas, who carried a pillow with rings until he stood next to Officer Dirk, who was dressed in a black-and-white tuxedo. The pastor went to the center of the gazebo between them and began the ceremony. I had never been so happy for a couple or so proud. I glanced over to the small crowd of about fifty people and saw some familiar faces. My parents were sitting together in the front row. They were beaming and, still surprisingly, were becoming friends again. When it got to the exchange of vows and rings, Officer Dirk had tears in his eyes and pledged not only to always care and love her but also Douglas with all his heart. My husband Louigi, who looked like a dream boat in his black-and-white tuxedo, handed Officer Dirk their wedding rings. It was an amazing day. The sun was shining. The people who attended were overcome with joy. In the second row, behind my parents, were Jack and Marla. She would probably be the next to get married, because she now sported a very large engagement ring on her fourth finger. Although Marla's face had a few scars from the vulture attacks, she was more beautiful than ever. Sitting next to Marla was my best friend Donna, who actually brought Snowflake, her white cat, in a pink dress inside a carrier. Suddenly, the pastor announced the new couple; the clapping noise became deafening, and even Doofus let out a bark with glee at my feet. Then he rushed over to Donna and wagged his tail at Snowflake. Snowflake jumped back in her carrier and, with squinty green eyes, showed Doofus her claws. Afterwards, a group of us gathered by the cake table set up on the porch.

"That's some cake Louigi made," Officer Dirk said looking down at the handcuffed bride on top and the groom dragging her away wearing a badge.

"My husband has a sense of humor." I hoped he really liked it.

"I love it," he said. Douglas rushed over.

"Daddy, how much longer?"

"He's calling you Daddy now?" I said, gladly.

"He does," Officer Dirk grinned. "I told him after the wedding we'd go back to his new playground for a while if he did a good job as ringbearer."

"And I did a great job!" Douglas boasted.

"Yes, you sure did!" Officer Dirk picked him up. Jack and Marla joined us.

"This is quite the set up," Jack shook Officer Dirk's hand.

"Yes, it is. Louigi and Laura went out of their way to make this so special." Officer Dirk released Jack's hand.

"Thanks again for helping build the playground for Douglas."

"No problem, thanks for getting me into the police academy."

"How's that going?" I asked him.

"Got A's on all my tests so far," Jack said.

"I had no idea how much studying goes in to learning all the codes and regulations."

"You'll do just fine," I told him.

"We know you'll have a job once you graduate."

"That's wonderful news," Donna said, clutching Snowflake's carrier and holding it up away from Doofus.

"We couldn't have one finer," Officer Dirk said.

"With you, I know you are willing to risk everything to save someone else and have our backs."

"He'll be one fine officer," Marla said.

"That's good that Jack has support," I mentioned to Marla.

"And how are you?"

"I am going to beauty school to become a cosmetologist," Marla announced. "I've always been into hair, make up, and nails. So, I thought I'd enjoy that. You also hear the best gossip as a hairdresser."

"I wish you both all the best in school," I said.

"It's hard work, but it pays off, and a degree or certificate is something no one can take away from you."

"We're gonna be just fine," Jack said.

"My father may not be able to come to my wedding next year, but my Uncle Michael will walk her down the aisle, and we are both leaving our gangs."

I glanced over and saw Michael asking my mother for a dance as the DJ began playing her favorite Frank Sinatra song "My Way." Many couples began to dance in the yard when the song began. My mother at first said yes, but my father took her hand away from Michael's and told him he could have the next one. Louigi carried a birdcage with two white doves in them from out of the house.

"I thought you said no birds?" Officer Dirk asked.

"May your love last forever," Louigi said. Officer Dirk wrapped his arm around Captain McBride as he held Douglas in his other arm.

"Amen to that."

We watched the two doves fly out of the cage. They circled one another a few times and then flew high in the cloudless, azure sky.

To make a donation to
St. Jude's Children's Hospital go to:
http://www.st.jude.org
St. Jude Children's Research Hospital